Territory

Dan Howarth

Northern Republic

Copyright © 2022 by Dan Howarth

All rights reserved. No part of this publication may be reproduced or transmitted in any form or by any means, electronic or otherwise, without written permission from the author.
This is a work of fiction. Any semblance to actual persons living or dead, businesses, events, or locales is purely coincidental.

Edited by Vicky Brewster.

Interior Formatting by Northern Republic.

Cover Art by Paul Stephenson at Hollow Stone Press.

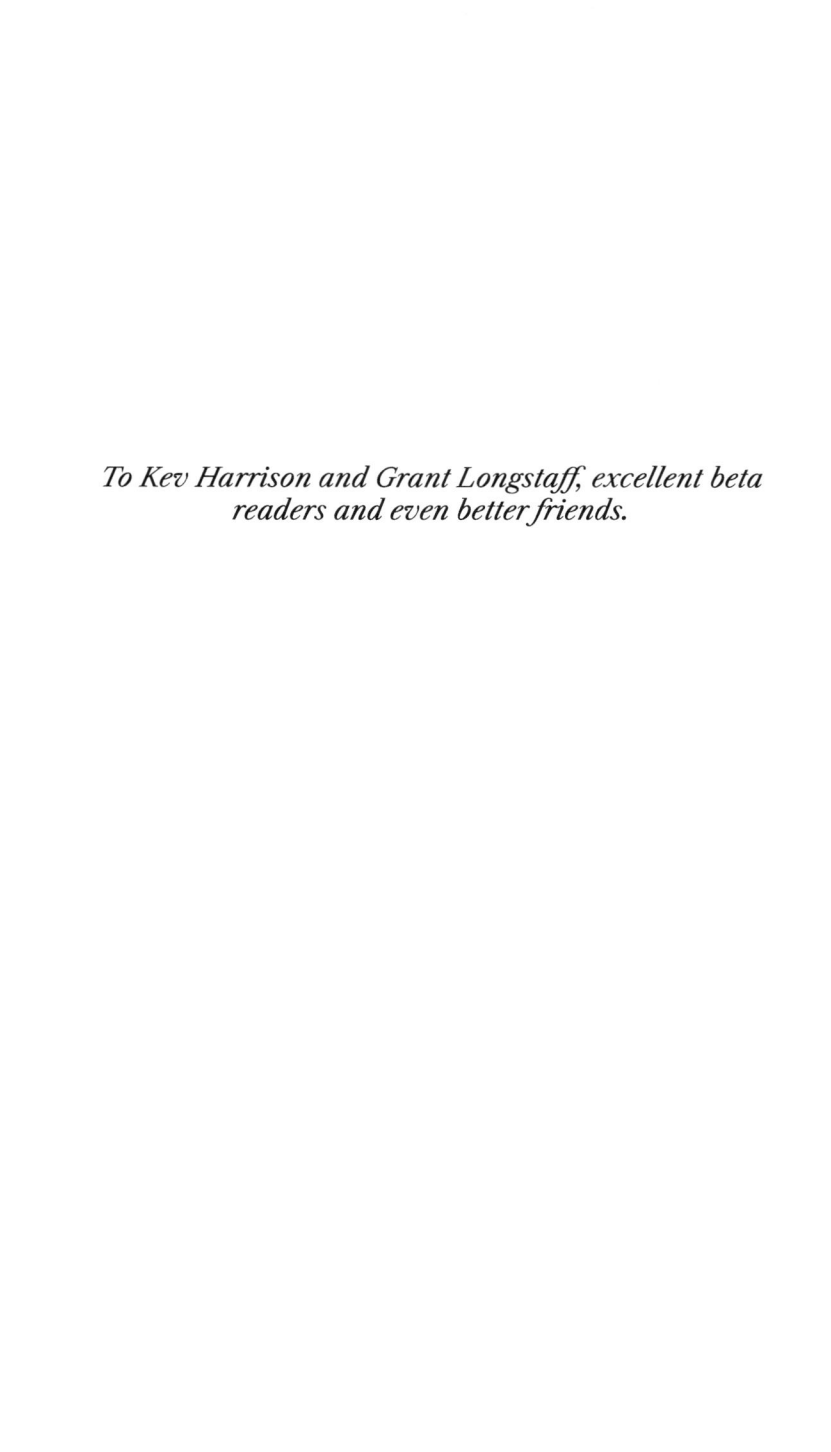

To Kev Harrison and Grant Longstaff, excellent beta readers and even better friends.

When that deep cold comes and settles into the land, of all the things to hibernate, the first is the kindness in a man's soul.

Contents

1. Chapter 1 — 1
2. Chapter 2 — 13
3. Chapter 3 — 21
4. Chapter 4 — 43
5. Chapter 5 — 53
6. Chapter 6 — 61
7. Chapter 7 — 73
8. Chapter 8 — 101
9. Chapter 9 — 115

Acknowledgements — 118
About The Author — 120
Also By Dan Howarth — 121

Chapter One

The scraping drags him from his vigil on the couch, as though the sound were inside his skull. Garish colours from the TV coat the walls of the room, alternately yellow and blue and red. A sitcom theme tune plays almost inaudibly, a jaunty whisper into the darkness. Jari sits up, unable to tell whether he's awake or asleep. His senses swim, struggling with time's corrosive touch, sapping his ability to recover.

Beer cans and the carcass of a microwave meal lie on the coffee table. Hassa stirs, her tail moving first, then she stretches, all muscle and sinew. Hassa's musk adds to the stale beer and leftover food. Despite the temperature outside, he longs to open the window. Clear his head.

His eyes open and close as he tries to focus. Four cans on the coffee table. He's had worse nights. Magda's picture looks at him from her frame above the television. It used to be that he thought her smile was down to joy, but now he looks up at her, broken and half pissed on the sofa, and he sees only sympathy in her face.

The scratching again. Louder this time. More insistent.

Hassa whines on the floor, and Jari looks down at his dog. She used to spend the nights outside, even nights like this one. Blacker than hell and colder than the grave. Even as the snow piled up, Hassa would stay tied to her post, sleeping in her cage.

Dogs are for hunting; they are not pets. They are not to be fussed over or domesticated. When you hunt for a living, dogs are partners. Part of a team. Nobody in that team can afford to be pampered or complacent. Nobody can afford to be soft.

But last night, he brought her in. Not because of the snow or the cold. Something deeper: instinct. After what happened with Lori, he doesn't want to take any chances. Nobody here can afford to lose anything else, be it dogs, livestock – he glances again at Magda – or family.

On cue, Hassa starts whining at his feet. He reaches down, eyes still on the TV, and feels her ears pinned back. Tension is taut in her muscles.

Again, the scraping outside. Something sharp digging in the snow, just the other side of the wall.

Silently, he finds the remote. Kills the TV. It plunges him into darkness apart from the phosphorous glow from the porch light outside which creeps around the edges of his curtains and through the sliver in the middle. Up here, darkness is an old acquaintance. Something that holds the village close in its long, tight embrace through the winter months. At this time of year, it steals the light earlier and earlier, suckling it from the sky like a greedy infant at a teat.

Tonight, there is no familiarity in the darkness. No comfort to be found.

Hassa growls in the blackness, and Jari imagines rather than sees bared teeth and black gums. Although she came to him as a replacement for Lori, she's proven herself over the last year. Whilst she could never truly replace the dog he'd reared from a pup, she tries her best.

In the darkness, he guides her away from the living room, shuts her in his bedroom. Alone and separated, she howls, the sound muted by the closed door.

His eyes adjust, and he half feels, half sees his way around the room, to the rifle he keeps by the front door.

Magda always hated this habit, hated seeing weapons on display. But to Jari, every action has a purpose.

He snatches up the rifle, already loaded. He cocks it. Trying to be as silent as possible despite Hassa's muffled yelps. He nudges the curtain open an inch. The porch light coats everything in yellow, like a faded photograph. Beyond the reach of the light is the forest, impenetrable and looming. The mouth of night's yawning cavern.

On the driveway, his truck stands sentry. Untouched. The path from the truck's driver's side to his porch is intact. Lori's old tether, now Hassa's, protrudes through the snow. Its shadow is black on the carpet of white.

The scratching again. The sound draws his eye as well as his ears.

Movement beneath the window. Scratching against the wall of the house, scraping on the snow. Snow flies backwards away from the house, piling a few feet away in clumps. He leans closer to the glass, ignoring the numbness of the chill on his cheek. Straining to see the source of the movement, he puts a hand against the pane and angles his face down.

The sound stops.

Without realising he's been holding his breath, he exhales, vapour fogs the frozen glass as two grey forms streak away from the house and towards the woods. He wipes the pane clean with his forearm to see two wolves slow to a trot at the boundary of his property, their initial hurry gone. Their bodies move with an athletic grace, a quiet power.

That they stop running concerns him. Their lack of fear gives rise to his own. They've come here for Hassa, just as they did for Lori. That they remembered this place, his home, makes him shudder and step back from the glass.

He keeps his eyes on the wolves but hopes to make it harder for them to see. They stop running, stand still and stare at his window. Their eyes reflect the porch light, shining yellow against the blackness of the night. Their fur is dark and wet in patches the snow has yet to cleanse. Their tongues loll, breath almost solid in the frozen night as they lick lips and teeth.

A thought prickles his conscience. Pierces the tiredness and rising headache. Stops everything else dead.

Is the noise for my benefit? Is it deliberate?

As Hassa yowls from his bedroom, a more tangible thought takes over.

They were hoping Hassa would escape.

He smiles, half pleased with himself for working it out and not falling for the trap. Unsettled that his conclusion is beyond everything he's learned about these animals. These vermin.

The means to this particular end rests in his hands. Calling to him. The reassurance of wood and metal. Manmade solutions to ancient problems.

Outside, the wolves moved as one. Their heads are cocked for movement and sound, muscles poised for fight or flight. Comfortable in their own dominion. Once the sun went down, man's world became theirs. With doors closed, fires blazing, curtains drawn against the outside world, the wolves are free to do what they want.

The village wakes to find the wreckage day on day.

Outside, the wolves turn their heads away from his house, ears raised to a sound that Jari can't hear. Their bodies relax at whatever they're hearing, heads hang. To Jari, it looks as though they are standing down. Wolves know their order within the pack. If these two are relaxing, it will be because of the presence of another animal, one higher within the pack.

The wolves look away again, and Jari squints into the darkness beyond them, craving movement. Desperate to see if his theory is correct. Still standing their ground at the edge of his land, the wolves continue to stare, heads half-cocked as though listening to advice.

This is his opportunity.

He backs away from the window and bumps into the sofa in the blackness of his living space. The curtain flops back into place, and he can't tell whether the wolves are still watching him or not. It doesn't matter. He has the element of surprise if he's quick.

In silence, he unbolts the door. All three locks slide open easily. He cradles the gun, calms his breathing. It's easy to miss a shot if panic is pulling the strings. He chews down his rage at these animals. The beasts that took Lori from him. The pack that terrorises his community.

He can't shoot straight like this. In his mind's eye, he sees a still, frozen lake. Breathes deeply. His heartbeat slows. He's ready.

Without looking out again, he wrenches open the front door and steps out onto the illuminated porch. Cold immediately assaults him, stealing the breath from his lungs and the feeling from his exposed face and hands. His slippers crunch into the snow, and freezing water drenches his feet.

He brings the rifle to his shoulder, his eye to the scope. He's alone.

Alone with only their footprints in the snow. He cups a hand above his eyes, shielding them from the light. In the darkness of the forest, he sees them move. Black on black. The pair of them run with the familiar, lolling gait of their kind. Side by side. Perhaps mates or, more likely, hunting partners.

He watches them go, far out of range already. He squints again, his eyes craving detail of the moving shapes in the forest. Unable to tell at this distance whether there are more out there. Hunter's instinct tells him there are always more out there. Always more of these insatiable animals waiting for their turn to feed.

A chill spreads up through his sodden feet and into his calves. It stirs his thoughts away from the wolves and back to more immediate concerns. He slams the door, fastens the locks, and double-checks them. Stashes his rifle back in its usual position by the door.

Hassa whines from his bedroom until he lets her out. She pushes through the gap before he's got it halfway open. As he feeds the fire, Hassa jumps up onto the sofa. Usually, this leads to her being shoved down onto the floor again, but not tonight.

Tonight, he's too grateful for her company. Grateful to himself for remembering to bring her in. When he takes his seat, she nuzzles him. Her nose is warm and wet against his shoulder.

Sleep isn't coming for him tonight. Even with daylight many hours away. Instead, he turns the TV back on. The familiar menu screen of the BBC sitcom. One of Magda's old favourites. He starts it from the beginning again, almost able to hear her laughter at the corny jokes. He keeps the English audio on, Finnish subtitles. He's done drinking for the night and holds on to the warmth of his dog as she starts to doze, head on his lap, both of them waiting for the dawn.

***

Snow covers the village and surrounding areas. A deep, white covering that bleaches the colour and the detail from everything it touches. Sharp edges and potholes await beneath its surface.

Jari kneels in the snow as the two other men watch him. His eyes scan the tracks and jagged cuts in the snow.

"It started with just the two of them, like you say, Asko." Jari takes a swig of coffee. It doesn't make a dent on the chill in his bones. "But by this point, I count eight."

"Eight? You're mistaken," Steffen, the third man, says.

"When has he ever been wrong?" Asko says.

Jari stands up. Shrugs. "I'm just telling it like I see it."

Without a word, the other two men follow him and the tracks away from the village and out into the forest.

***

Wolf tracks skirt the lines of every villager's property, but from what Jari can tell, they were most brazen at his house. A site where the pack have killed before. He looks up to the sky at the thought of Lori's blood.

Out in the forest, the scene changes. The signs of the chase become more obvious. Broken branches and trenches of carved-up snow, revealing scrub grass and mud beneath the brilliant white. A mile from the site, the other wolves joined in the chase. They spotted the first pool of red snow.

As the three most experienced hunters in the village, Jari, Asko and Steffen took ownership of tracking the wolves. Not at the request of the other villagers, but because it came naturally to them. An instinctive action.

More stained snow comes into view, the stains wider and the colour deeper. The lifeblood of some poor animal frozen into the snow. Jari pulls his rifle from his shoulder and turns off the safety. Without a word, the others follow suit. They advance through the silent forest. Breath steams in front of their faces.

Sound travels out here, away from the rush of the cities and towns. Some days, Jari can hear his neighbours' children playing the better part of a mile away.

But today, he hears nothing. The village and the forest keep a sombre vigil.

Cold rises in his lower back as he realises there's no birdsong. Something has silenced the forest's ubiquitous choir. As he's trained himself to do, he calms his breathing to ensure any shots he takes are true.

Now he leads them, rifle first, along the increasingly bloody trail.

He reaches the clearing and lowers his rifle without taking his eyes from the scene; signals to the others to do the same.

The clearing is a butcher's floor.

Only Asko can stand to take a second look. Jari and Steffen turn their faces away. Hunter's pride forgotten in the face of nature's fury. Their eyes comb the blank, white snow for comfort against what they have just seen.

The moose is now a pile, a heap of cracked bone and half-chewed gristle. What's left of it lies on its side, hollowed out, muscle and organ alike devoured. Nicotine-yellow ribs jut out, jagged and broken. Its fur sags, torn and discarded. Its eye, exposed within the socket, stares up at the clear sky. The scene reeks of punctured bowels and old blood.

"I've never seen anything like this before," Steffen says. His voice is thick behind his snood. "Fucking eight of them doing this to an animal." He turns to face the scene as though checking his vision hasn't played a trick on him. He turns away again. "This is too much."

"One of them is too much," Jari says. He steels himself and turns back to the scene, more disgusted with his own weakness than anything he's looking at. He forces himself not to turn away. "They've got braver. They ran this poor creature down for miles. It must've been dead on its feet."

"Sammi won't take this well when he hears," Steffen says. "He's already in the shit with the bank."

"Who isn't?" Jari says, his eyes finding Asko. Both men grunt their agreement. "The question is, what do we do next? People need to know what's going on. Starting with Sammi."

"Sammi is a different issue. People know what's happening here – they're just choosing to ignore it. They don't want to have to make the difficult decisions," Steffen says.

"It'll be out of their hands soon enough when we're scraping a person off the snow."

"Wait a minute," Asko says, one huge, gloved hand raised. "There's nothing to say that's how this ends."

"That's exactly how this ends," Steffen says. His voice is too loud for the silent forest. "More and more livestock. That's the escalation. Then it's a person. You can't deny this isn't where it's all heading."

"Where it's heading is a rash decision. Next thing, you'll be charging off into the woods hunting wolves alone."

"I'm angry. I'm not stupid. And neither is anyone else in this village."

Jari puts a hand up, cutting between the two other men as they stare each other down. "Calm down. Both of you. There's no easy fix to this situation. These wolves are a community problem. The village needs to make its own decision based on the facts that we have. Not on speculation."

Both Asko and Steffen try to speak at the same time. Jari cuts them off.

"Right now, what we need to do is get out of here. To clear our heads and think rationally about what we do next. If we get het up on bloodlust then we're no better than these animals."

"So you're taking his side?" Steffen says, turning to Jari.

"It's not about sides, is it? It's about the right decision. After Lori was torn apart by these bastard things, you think I didn't want to kill every one of them? I still do. But there's ways and means. You do things right."

"And what's the right thing to do? Bring Sammi out here so he can see exactly what happened to his animal worth hundreds of euros?"

"Nobody else needs to see this until the right time. People are nervous. They need to be cautious and careful, not frothing at the mouth for revenge or cowering in their homes. When people are angry and frightened, they get careless."

"And what about if someone finds this? Are we going to spend the day cleaning it up?"

"Nobody will find it. There's no reason to come here. Leave it."

"I agree," Asko says. "But people need to see this for themselves."

He pulls out his phone, fumbling with it, gloved fingers clumsy and slow. With one bare hand, he snaps pictures. Camera shutter sounds fill the air as he moves around the scene, like a CSI photographer. Jari watches his friend step between bone and blood, Asko's movements are those of a man much smaller in stature.

"That's enough," Jari says. "We want to inform people, not terrify them."

Asko nods, walks back to where the three of them now stand, overlooking the carnage.

"Those pictures stay on your phone until the time's right, OK? Not a word about this to anyone until I say so." Jari looks first at Asko then to Steffen. Both men nod their agreement, faces hidden by snoods and sunglasses.

"What should I tell Sammi?" Steffen asks. "I'll go and see him on the way home."

"He needs to know the animal is dead. That's all. Beyond that, the details remain between us until we need to make a decision."

"And when will that be?"

"We'll know, but we're not far off if this pattern continues."

Without waiting to hear any more, Jari turns and trudges through the snow towards the village. Whilst tracking the trail left by the wolves and their prey, the three moved quickly, adrenaline flowing. Their walk back towards the village stretches out in front of them, longer somehow, their bodies bent against the cold.

Near the village, Steffen says his goodbyes. He leaves their path to visit Sammi's farm on the way home. Jari watches him, relieved to be left alone with Asko and not to have to witness Sammi's fury first-hand. His grief over Lori still smoulders, and there's no desire to reignite it until it becomes necessary.

Jari and Asko watch Steffen's form recede into the trees, disappearing as he navigates an incline away from them.

"Should we go after him?" Jari asks. "We shouldn't let anyone go out alone right now."

"They're long gone. Don't worry. Steffen can handle himself."

Asko isn't wrong. In the forty years he's known Steffen, he can barely remember the man missing a shot.

Asko watches Jari stare out into the forest. Silence envelops them.

Jari shakes his head; turns to Asko. The bigger man reaches down and pats Jari on the shoulder.

"Come on," Asko says. "Let's get going. It'll be dark soon."

Jari grimaces. "Round here, it's always dark soon."

Chapter Two

The apple-red truck sits idling outside Jari's house, its paint job a shock of colour against the canvas of the snow. It puts Jari in mind of the clearing. A gentle thrum of bass punctuates the silence of the woods. Emissions float up from the exhaust, though the engine runs almost soundlessly.

Jari looks from the brand-new Hilux to his own truck, buried by the front door, grateful for the snow covering the dints and scratches. Next to him, Asko breaks into a smile that's noticeable even behind his snood and glasses.

"She must want to know how it went." Asko picks up his pace and is at a clumsy half-jog through the snow by the time Jari catches up with him. His hand finds his friend's elbow, stopping him.

"Be careful what you tell her about all this."

"She's my wife. I tell her everything."

"Then tell her to be careful about what she says to the others."

"Which others?"

"The other women, the other wives. Whoever she socialises with."

Asko scratches the back of his head. "I don't think that's an issue, Jari. She's still finding it hard to settle. You know how these small communities are. It's different to Helsinki."

"I'm sorry, Asko. You should've said. I'm sure if Magda were here, then she would've ..."

"I'm sure she would've helped too."

"Why don't you both come in for some coffee? I might even be able to find a biscuit."

"Sure. We'd like that."

***

Jari races into the house whilst Asko greets Pia at the door. In a frenzy, he sweeps up last night's beer cans and breaks his own rule, stashing his rifle out of sight. Nothing screams paranoia like a firearm easily to hand. The kitchen and living room adjoin. Jari plumps the sofa cushions and wipes down the kitchen sides. It's presentable, if not immaculate. He doesn't live in squalor, but as Jari and Pia enter the house, he knows it still smells of grief.

He gets the coffee going on the stove, the last of the expensive stuff he'd had posted from relatives in the city. Their note asking him to visit has long since been consigned to the bin. Pia and Asko kick their boots off and remove their outer layers. Hands held, they take the sofa. Released from the bedroom, Hassa runs over to them, tongue out, tail wagging. For the moment, she's not the trained worker Jari has strived for, but a daft, instinctive dog.

Hassa prostrates herself in front of Asko as he rubs her belly, legs in the air. Pia reaches forward to join in, but Hassa scrambles to her feet and clacks over the kitchen tiles to where Jari is stood.

"You dozy sod, play nice. She's Asko's wife, you're not."

"Can't blame the girl for trying. Look at this hunk of man." Pia throws her arms around Asko. Behind his dark beard, his smile widens, but he hesitates in hugging her back. His eyes meet Jari's before he looks away.

Jari turns back to the stove, the third wheel in his own home. He takes a breath and pours coffee. This is the closest he's come to entertaining guests for a long time, so he makes a point of remembering how they take their drinks.

On the couch, Pia's face is turned down to the floor. After delivering their drinks and a plate of spiced biscuits, Jari encourages Hassa to give Pia another try. After a few moments of Pia's petting, the dog scrambles up onto Asko, curling up on his lap.

"Bloody idiot dog." Jari sips his coffee, hoping he can get another delivery from his relatives without suffering their emotional blackmail.

"This is the good stuff," says Asko. "And you found biscuits, what a gentleman."

"It's a rare day there's something sweet leftover in this house."

Pia takes a biscuit and nibbles it with teeth that shine white like the snow outside. Jari watches her cup her hand under her chin to catch any crumbs. It's a sharp contrast to his last guest, Steffen, who drank Jari's beer without thanks and sat farting on his couch all night. It makes him smile behind his coffee mug.

"How was the tracking?" Pia asks.

The two men exchange a look over the tops of their cups.

"Not good," Jari says.

"It was a bloodbath," Asko says. His words all running together, as though he couldn't keep them in any longer.

"Were there many elk?"

"Just one," Jari says, eyes on Asko.

"They butchered it. Eight of them tore it to shreds," Asko says.

"But we aren't in the business of telling the details," Jari says, gaze unmoved.

"You said I could. Pia is part of this community now and won't say anything to anyone else until the time is right."

"I'm sat right here, Asko. I can speak for myself."

"Your call then." Jari sips his coffee, bites into a biscuit with a crisp snap, watches the couple as they face each other.

"What happened in that clearing is unlike anything I've ever seen. The carnage, the fury. That animal never stood a chance. The wolves chased it down for a long time. They killed it slowly through exhaustion and loss of blood. After that, they dismantled it. This wasn't just for food. It was sport for them." Asko's breathless by the time he finishes.

"And that's not normal?" Pia turns to Jari. "Sorry. In Helsinki, wolves are nothing but a fairy tale. We know they exist, but they're only in zoos or children's books for us."

"No need to apologise. It takes time to adjust to our way of life," Jari says, wondering how long it will take when she's already been here a year or more.

"It's a cause for concern more than anything. It means they're getting bolder," Asko says.

Jari sits forward. "I saw two of them last night. Must've been before the chase started. Digging at the front of my house. Right by Lori's post." He shakes his head. "Hassa's post. Right up against the wall of the house. Looking for food probably, but at the same time, it was like they were trying to wake me." He finishes his coffee. "Or get in."

Pia puts a hand over her mouth and turns to Asko. The big man shakes his head, pulls her in close. On his lap, Hassa grunts and jumps down. Asko's eyes remain on Jari, his brows bent into a frown.

"But as I've said, that they're killing our livestock isn't really *their* fault. If Sammi can't protect his own herds, then that's his problem when he can't afford to pay the bills."

"Maybe," Jari says. "I feel bad for the man, but yes, he needs to take some responsibility for his own herd. My real problem is how bold the wolves are now. Coming closer to the village every night. Waiting for dark and doing what they want. They're not scared of us anymore."

Pia straightens up from Asko's hug. Picks up her cup again. "What do you think we should do then, Jari? As a community."

"It's not for me to speak for everyone, but if I had my way, we'd have culled them all when they took Lori. I'd have killed every single one of them and made them into coats and rugs."

He smiles, but nobody laughs.

"But killing wolves because they wronged you, that's not what we're talking about here."

"No. It's about the economics of the situation for people like Sammi, but it's a safety issue as well. We're already taking measures to keep people safe. What next? We can't go out after dark anymore?"

"There's no evidence that the wolves would hurt someone?"

"You would say that. You didn't see what they did to that elk. Have a look at the pictures when you get home — I've no interest in seeing them again."

"An elk and a person are very different."

"In our eyes perhaps, but to them, we're all the same. Sooner or later, we're all just meat."

Pia's eyes shine with tears. She turns to Asko, who squeezes her hand before he speaks.

"It won't come to that. If it gets any worse, we'll talk to the villagers. Decide on what to do next. Speak to the government if necessary."

"Helsinki doesn't give a shit about what we do out here. They think we're half-Russian as it is. You heard it yourself just now: wolves are just fairy tales in the city. More to the point, they're someone else's problem. Ours."

"Maybe, but it's not for you to decide alone, Jari."

"Maybe not. But I'll take any action I see necessary to protect my land from now on. I don't need Helsinki or anyone else to tell me that."

Jari bites his lip after speaking, wanting something to do with his hands and regretting putting down his empty cup. His knuckles crack as they whiten. His temper rising again, getting him in trouble. He looks away from the couple on his sofa. Chews harder on his lip.

"I'm sorry," Asko says. "I know after Lori and with the other things going on ... it can't be easy right now. But I want what's best for the village too. Last thing I want is good friends being hauled off to jail for culling wolves or accidentally shooting someone."

Jari smiles at this. "You're more likely to do that than anyone, Asko. You're out of practice."

Asko shrugs. "A bit of time in the city hasn't rubbed the village off me totally, Jari. You can rely on me."

Pia reaches down in another unsuccessful attempt to rub Hassa's belly. The dog stands up, jumps on Jari's lap.

"Come on, Asko, we need to get going and try to fix the second truck today before it gets dark." She looks over at Jari and Hassa. "Thanks for the coffee. We'd love you to come over for a meal one night. Perhaps talk about something other than wolves?" She smiles, and so does Jari. He nods his approval.

Pia gets her outside clothes and boots on first, says her goodbyes, and leaves the two friends together as Asko pulls on his boots. He towers over Jari, just as he always has.

"We don't live in the city, Jari. We have our own traditions out here. We have our own duty to sustain the environment. Make it safe for us and our kids. Give them something to live on and live for in the future. Wolves are part of that whether you like them or not."

"We're hunters, Asko. It's how most of us survive."

"Hunters. Not butchers."

They look at each other in silence. Jari's chin turns up to meet Asko's gaze.

"It's been a while since we've had a beer together," Asko says. "Let's put that right one night, OK?"

Without waiting for a response, Asko steps out into the bite of the afternoon air and shuts the front door behind, leaving Jari alone with Hassa.

Chapter Three

Lotta turns the TV down and cocks her head, hearing Kandi's yips and barks over the racket of the soap opera she watches twice a day every day. She gets up from her chair. At eye level, above the fireplace, is a picture of her late father. Stern features belie his soft laugh and gentle nature. His moustache gives him a gentrified look and hides his missing teeth. Ten years gone. Ten years in the ground.

Kandi runs into the living room, jumping up and barking. Lotta sighs at these mannerisms, flaws she's worked hard on training out of the dog. For the most part, she's succeeded, but Kandi's temperament makes her lose her discipline when she's excited. It's not caused them any mishaps when hunting, not yet.

Lotta opens the door, and Kandi nudges her way through, all head and shoulders. Opening the door wider, Lotta steps out of the way so her dog can rush past. Kandi scampers out onto the snow-covered patio.

"Be careful," Lotta finds herself muttering as Kandi skids over the buried concrete slabs and into a bush covered in snow. As though composing herself, Kandi shakes the snow from her fur and trots onto the lawn, where the snow is deeper.

Lotta keeps the door open for as long as she can before the chill steals the feeling from her fingers and face. In the warmth of the kitchen, she gets to work at the sink, washing and peeling potatoes at a place where she can keep eyes on Kandi.

Trees line the back garden of her property, creating a natural border between her land and the wild forest behind it. Snow doesn't fall as heavily at the back of her house as at the front – the fir trees provide shelter from the elements. Her nearest neighbours, Steffen and Helenka, are far enough away not to be intrusive, but the pines provide a wall of green between them and her.

Kandi yips and barks on the lawn, chasing her tail and jumping around in the snow that falls gently but insistently. She jumps to catch flakes and chases those taken by the breeze. Every movement and every scent provide stimulus after a morning spent inside.

Amused by what she's seen, Lotta finds Kandi's favourite chew toy, opens the back door, and launches it out into the snow. She smiles from the window as Kandi shakes the toy from side to side, her teeth buried in the rubber.

On the kitchen side, a haunch of venison rests. Lotta presses her fingers into the meat, feeling that it's reached room temperature. She sets the kettle on the hob and boils some water. Checks the time on her father's watch around her wrist. She still has four hours before Jari is due. Time enough to cook the meal and to get changed. She pauses by the meat, hands on hips, and tries to decide whether roasting the meat will be enough to impress. Although it imparts flavour, does it display enough effort, enough care? In the time she's known Jari – mostly since his wife passed away – he doesn't seem as though he'd care whether the meat was roasted or not. She sticks to her guns, piling onions and garlic onto the roasting tray with the meat, and puts it into the oven.

She moves to the sink, hands on hips to watch Kandi play. Concentric circles of footprints carve up the snow on the lawn. Erratic patterns mix the lines. Kandi's chew toy lies discarded. The dog herself is still, staring into the woods at something Lotta cannot see.

A streak of piss behind Kandi turns the snow yellow and melts a small trench into the powder.

Lotta wipes away the condensation from the pane and cups her hand against the glass to better see out into the afternoon grey. Her eyes scan the trees, but there's no movement, no sign of whatever is fixating her dog. Straining, she tries to listen, but the boiling kettle and humming oven are too loud.

She shakes her head and washes some herbs ready to be chopped. She's spent her whole life around dogs. Living with them, working with them, training them. All her earliest memories involve a dog, usually her father's favourite, Heinz. She smiles at the thought of the gentle dog many decades dead. Although she's spent her life training dogs, there's still a wild streak within them she's never mastered. Never fully controlled. Perhaps they always sensed that deep down, she'd rather be somewhere else, doing something else.

She frowns now at that wild streak, as her dog begins to move slowly on the snow. That Kandi has marked her territory in this way isn't unusual, but irritation fills Lotta that she can't see what's sparked this behaviour.

She pours the boiling water into the pan with the potatoes and adds salt. The pan gurgles and comes to a rolling boil. Satisfied, she fills the sink and begins to wash the pots. Between dishes, she looks up, eyes keen for Kandi's form, hoping to see her playing again.

Kandi is still on the lawn, a trail of shit in the snow behind her now.

Lotta follows the dog's gaze and drops the metal dish she's cleaning. It clangs onto the floor, unnoticed.

A wolf stands at the end of her garden.

Yards from Kandi, its languid form is a shock of grey against the growing shadow of the trees. Its yellow eyes are fixed on the dog.

Although Lotta has seen and killed bigger wolves in the past, the predator still dwarfs Kandi. The chew toy dangles from the wolf's jaws, a hypnotic movement.

Her lungs scream for air, and she gasps it in.

Outside, the wolf withdraws into the forest.

Lotta scrambles to the back door, wrenches it open. Cold air rushes in, greedy to get inside the house.

"Kandi," she calls. Her voice carries no weight in the face of the trees crowding the garden.

Kandi continues to stare into the woods.

Lotta whistles, the usual call to Kandi to come to heel. Kandi doesn't flinch, doesn't turn.

"Kandi." Louder now.

"Kandi!" A strain in her voice, a change in pitch.

Kandi doesn't look back before trotting between two pine trees and disappearing into the darkness beneath the forest canopy.

"Kandi!" One last attempt at discipline. Hysteria warbles through her voice.

She waits. Kandi doesn't return.

Without thinking, Lotta steps out onto the veranda. Ankle-high snow seizes her slippered feet, soaking them in its freezing grasp. Lotta gasps against the cold and carries on across the veranda and the lawn. She skirts the area where Kandi soiled herself, struggling for grip in her inappropriate footwear.

Lotta approaches the trees, squinting into the darkness. Around her, light is draining from the sky as early afternoon gives in to rapacious night. Already the snow is grey, drained of its daytime sheen. Her hand finds one of the pines, propping her up as she leans forward into the forest, shouting Kandi's name over and over.

Silence greets her.

She takes a step between the trees, her footing more secure where less snow can infiltrate between the branches. Her hand still on the tree, she pauses. She takes a breath, lets her thoughts solidify. Tries to take the emotion out of the situation. Brings back the experience of hunting, all the lessons she learned from her family over the years. Imagines the scorn of her uncles and her father for charging into the woods without boots.

Without a weapon.

Cold tells her to go home. Whispers into her bones that she is not up to this challenge.

She ploughs back across the garden, into the house. Through the kitchen and into the living room. Her movements echo through the furniture as her haste makes her clumsy.

The gun cabinet on the wall screams at her. She pulls down the first rifle her hand comes to. Her father's. She loads it. Stuffs extra shells into the pockets of her jeans. Slips her feet into her boots but doesn't tie them. There's no time for more layers. There's no time to retrieve her weapon really, but needs must. Without it, she'll be too vulnerable.

She thunders through the kitchen and out across the garden, back to the spot where Kandi disappeared between the trees. Even in the moment that's passed since she stepped inside, the world seems darker, quieter. As though turning her back for a second has made her more isolated.

She puts a hand on one of the pines, its bark sticky beneath her fingers as she steadies herself to step beyond the two trees that Kandi disappeared between. *A successful hunt comes from staying calm.* Messages drummed into her by her father and uncles on hunting trips as a young girl. To go charging in never results in anything other than failure.

Snow crunches beneath her boots, a light dusting. Under the canopy of the trees, snow lingers on the tips of branches and roots rather than drowning them as it does elsewhere.

A breeze whispers through the trees, making smaller branches judder and a prickle crawl across her scalp.

No coat. No hat. No gloves. She's rushed in. She tries once again to calm her breathing, to remain in control. Although she's not come prepared, she still has her skills and, if she stays calm, her wits.

The barrel of her rifle leads the way from this point. Lotta's eyes scan the tracks on the group. Kandi's smaller, almost dainty prints and a patchwork of larger prints. They lead her away from her home, away from safety, and deeper into the forest where daylight is losing its daily battle with the night.

The foliage thins, and the tracks on the ground reveal more of themselves. Kandi's prints are deeper, as though running through the snow. To the right of her tracks, the prints of the wolf. Lotta pauses and squints. There are too many footprints in the snow for just two animals. The wolf's tracks double up, the stride length cut in half as though two animals walked single file together through this point.

Numb fingers tighten on the handle of her rifle. She never keeps the safety on. Rifles are tools, not weapons. They are treated with respect, cleaned and maintained to the highest standard. Out here, a jammed rifle can be the difference between life and death. In her hands, the wood and metal give her reassurance, familiarity.

Concern for Kandi drives her forward. Her thoughts jump to the scene she might find. Premature grief gnaws a hole in her mind that even her growing fear cannot fill quickly enough.

Two wolves. She breathes deeply.

Every hunting party she's ever been part of has outnumbered its prey at least two to one. Now the shoe is on the other foot. The odds of this hunt have changed; they are not in her favour. She bites her lip and clutches the rifle tighter. Her equaliser.

Silence has the forest in a chokehold. Lotta cocks her head to one side, straining for a sound. No birds sing. No animals move around her. After a few seconds of holding still, she doesn't want to move again, aware that every step she takes is broadcast to listening ears. There is no choice, and she starts to walk again. Tentative steps and deliberate movements. Eyes wide and alert. The rifle out, ready to shoot.

Kandi yips somewhere up ahead.

The sound makes Lotta jump, her numb fingers closing tighter on the rifle. Her heart thrashes and then settles, thundering a different rhythm now she knows Kandi is still alive. That was her usual bark, a playful yip that she lets out in excitement. There's a chance, albeit slim, that Kandi will get out of this in one piece.

There's a chance that they both will.

Despite the ache in her chest, she remains methodical in her movements. Steps slow and careful, not rushing. A twist of an ankle or a strained knee ligament in this place could be curtains. She's already far enough from home that nobody would hear her shouts for days.

She swings around at that thought, as though feeling eyes on her. The path she's made through the foliage is empty. Above her, a blackbird sits and watches in silence. A mute spectator. It makes no attempt to move or to sing, subdued by the presence beneath it. Lotta swallows. It isn't her the bird is afraid of.

Kandi bursts into more yips. Lotta crouches and follows the sound. Bent this low, snow pours from the branches onto her, soaking into her thin fleece top and jeans. Her sodden hair hangs in her face. She sweeps it back and out of her eyes.

Another bark. And another.

She's close now. Her teeth clench together against the cold and in determination to save Kandi. Now she's close to the wolf, it's time to see this through and take out the predator. She pauses and looks down the rifle's sights. All in perfect order. As usual.

Behind a waist-high blackberry bush, she pauses. Hidden from view, she supports herself with one hand and peers over the top of the spindles and twigs.

In the small, scrubbed clearing ahead, Kandi stands by the wolf she saw in the garden. The two animals face away from where Lotta crouches, their faces turned and staring towards a darker, thicker section of the woods. Lotta squints, trying to follow the path of their vision, she sees nothing but endless greens and browns and blacks.

The wolf towers over Kandi. Up close, it is bigger than she suspected. Its sleek, athletic frame is lined with muscle. Matted blood beneath its chin from an earlier feast. Everything about it built to kill.

Her mind on the second set of tracks, she scans around, looking for the wolf's companion and seeing nothing. There are more birds in the trees here. Families of them watching her with small black eyes, impassive to the fate of the creatures below them. Regardless of what happens, they will sing again.

Her hands shake on the rifle, and she can't focus solely on the animals in front of her. Paranoia has her convinced that the second she raises the rifle to shoot, another wolf will come crashing through the undergrowth and tear into her.

She trains the rifle on the clearing. The wolf and Kandi have turned away from whatever they were looking at. The chew toy dangles from the wolf's mouth still. Kandi's head moves from side to side, mimicking the motion of the toy. Kandi moves closer to the wolf, blocking Lotta's clean shot of the predator.

Away to the side of the clearing, where the two animals were staring, there's a snap of a twig and a rustle of the undergrowth. Lotta trains her rifle on the area, hoping to take out the second wolf, but there's nothing there. Neither the wolf nor Kandi have turned towards the sound. They continue their game in the clearing. Kandi still watches the chew toy swing from side to side as though hypnotised.

There's a second snapping twig from the far side of the clearing. At this noise, the wolf drops the chew toy. With a bark, Kandi dances forward to retrieve it from between the wolf's feet. As she nears, the wolf watches until Kandi bends her head to pick up the toy. With her neck exposed, the wolf swoops down in one movement. Its jaws clamp around Kandi's neck and twist. In the silence of the forest, the sound of cracking bones rattles from tree to tree.

"No!" Lotta's on her feet, her voice keening and strained.

Shock steals her coordination, and she fumbles with the rifle. The wolf doesn't wait. It runs from Kandi's prone body and leaps away between two trees. Lotta tries and fails to locate it in the rifle sights. She takes her chances and fires blind. Bark explodes from a tree near to the wolf but the animal escapes, bounding away into the darkness. The sound of the shot cracks from tree to tree, shattering the blanket of silence.

Lotta runs into the clearing, panting after only a few steps. Rifle against her shoulder, she scans the darkness for movement, for anything to vent her fury on. Instead, she sees nothing other than trees and snow. She's alone.

Lowering her weapon, she turns to Kandi. The dog's body lies prone in the shallow snow of the clearing. Lying on its side, Kandi's head turns the wrong way, up towards the sky. Eyes look at the canopy of tree limbs they can no longer see. Her jaws are still clamped around her favourite toy.

Her rifle falls from her hands into the snow, and she sinks to her knees. Snow soaks her legs as tears fall onto her cheeks, stinging in the chill. Her heart thunders in her chest, as though going through its final motions before self-destructing, priming itself for an explosion.

She reaches down and rubs Kandi behind the ear with shaking fingers. The dog's skin is still warm beneath her frozen touch. Fur as soft as it always was. She reaches over and closes Kandi's eyes, unable to bear their lack of movement and comprehension. A sob escapes her, a deep guttural sound that grows, prolongs itself into a wail.

Scooping up snow as well as her friend, Lotta lifts Kandi into her arms, clutching her close to her chest one last time. Struggling with one hand, she retrieves her rifle from the snow, barrel pointed at the ground though it's tempting, briefly, in this moment, to raise it towards her own face. But she won't. Not today.

The cold greets her like an old friend as she trudges home. It drapes an arm around her shoulders, guiding her way along the funeral march. Above her, a bird bursts into song. Cheerful notes, no longer appealing or appropriate. Birdsong grows in volume and mocks her retreat to her own land, away from the dominion of nature.

Behind her, twigs crack and the foliage rustles. Up in the trees, the birds stop singing. Lotta breaks into a jog, head half-turned to look over her shoulder. She sees nothing as she stumbles over divots and potholes covered by snow and shrubbery. Spindly branches whip at her ankles.

A breaking twig up ahead. A crisp snap of wood. Loud. Deliberate.

No movement in the snow or between the trees.

Lotta doesn't stop. She puts her head down and charges towards her own property. She's stumbling, trying to sprint but weighed down by grief. Panting breaths freeze in her chest, making her lungs ache despite the short distance covered.

She bursts back into her garden. Almost sobs at the sight of her home. Snow falls in relentless droves. It's already covered Kandi's tracks from earlier, obliterating the record of her from the lawn. Lotta trudges on, barely lifting her feet over the level of the snow, creating trenches in the powder as she drags her feet.

She looks back over her shoulder, expecting to see a wolf chasing her across the lawn. But the trees stretch up as high as they ever have, dwarfing her and her home. Darkness continues its hostile takeover, stealing the colour and the detail from the world as it drags the cover of night over everything. She is alone.

Lotta thunders into the house, slams the door behind her and collapses against it, sinking to the floor. Free from her grip, the rifle clatters onto the linoleum, and a swell of hysterical laughter bubbles in her chest at the thought of it going off and blowing a hole in the cupboards.

A sob stifles the laughter as she looks down at Kandi's face, sobering her thoughts. The chew toy is gone, dropped and discarded in Lotta's flight back to the house. She pictures it lying in the snow, covered and forgotten. Kandi's most cherished possession, now ownerless. Kandi's mouth hangs open, her curved teeth stained yellow in black gums. Pink tongue lolling.

There will be no more hunts, no more treats for a job well done. And despite what her father would think about petting and rewarding the dog too much, no nights spent on the sofa together, sharing each other's warmth and company.

Tears flow in earnest then. Lotta hangs her head, and the tears slide from her face down onto Kandi's fur. In the movies she loved as a kid, this would bring her friend back to life. The scene would end with the dog jumping up and licking her face. There would be laugher and smiles. But this is not a movie. This is her life, and now she must lead it alone, robbed of her colleague and her companion.

She doesn't know how long she has been sat by the door when she starts to smell smoke. It's a tickle on the edge of her grief at first, dismissed in a breath but then more persistent. It stops her tears and the wracking of her chest. Carefully, she places Kandi on the mat by the back door and stands up.

A tendril of black smoke rises from the pan on the stove. She screams and turns it off. The potatoes have boiled dry and caught in the aluminium pan, burned black to the bottom of it. She screams again, lifts the pan from stove and launches it against the back wall of the kitchen. The metal clangs off the surface, leaving a scar in the wood as it thuds to the floor. Charred potatoes tumble out.

She leans on the kitchen side, putting her weight on it as she splashes cold water on her face at the sink. Another scream builds inside her, but she swallows it down. More mess and more destruction won't help her now. It won't bring Kandi back.

Lotta stares at her reflection in the pane. Beyond it, in the growing darkness, something moves. She leans closer. Wipes away traces of condensation. Squints out across the garden. A dark shape lingers on the fringes of her vision, as though it knows how far she can see and has purposely stood on the cusp of this distance. She senses rather than sees its form, the bestial nature of it.

As quickly as she can, she flips the switch for the patio lights and runs back to the window. The garden is illuminated in brilliant white, crystal clear under the LED lighting. A layer of perfect, undisturbed snow covers everything. In the shadows of the forest behind, there is only stillness.

Nothing moves. Nothing is caught unawares by the light. Nothing retreats into the depths of the forest.

She sighs and turns the lights off again, content that she imagined whatever she saw in the forest. As she returns to the kitchen, a blanket in her hands to wrap up Kandi's body, she pauses, head cocked to one side.

What happened to the second wolf?

She straightens up, the blanket dangling onto the floor. After hunting and tracking most of her life, she's confident in her own abilities. She's earned her living hunting and trapping for long enough to be certain she saw two sets of wolf tracks in the forest.

The feeling of being watched in the forest comes back to her and brings a shudder. The vulnerability of being outnumbered. She scratches the back of her head, paces the distance between the living room and the kitchen. She catches herself looking at the photograph of her father. His eyes chastise her for rushing into a dangerous situation.

She made a mistake today. That realisation is petrol on the fire of her panic. She shouldn't be thinking about the second wolf because she should've taken care of business properly. When the chance came to finish the wolf, it should've been second nature. She let emotions get in the way of her actions – something that she mustn't do again.

In the kitchen, she scoops up Kandi in the blanket and folds it over. She takes the corpse to the spare bedroom and places it on her mother's old dressing table. She refuses to catch her own eye in the attached mirror.

As she is about to sit down, there's a knock on the door. She looks up at the clock. Panic flushes her chest again, its impact lessened now. It's time to eat.

"Just a second," she calls as she smooths her hair back into a ponytail. Her jeans and fleece top are still damp in patches, muddy in others. Blood clouds the sleeves of her top. As usual, she's wearing no makeup. But there's no time for anything. Jari's here and likely hungry.

Kandi lies dead in another room, and despite her intentions for Jari, Lotta can't tear her thoughts away from her lost companion. She wipes her eyes on the back of her hands and opens the front door.

Jari stands on the front porch, wrapped against the cold, a bottle of whisky clutched in front of him like a weapon. He's smiling as she opens the door, which is unusual for him. But his expression reverts to normal as his eyes meet hers, his features a closed book.

"What's happened?"

She shakes her head and waves him inside, aware of the cold. He steps past her, kicking off his snow-caked boots and walking into the living room. She covers her face with one hand. It's taken so much work to get Jari here for this meal, even just as friends. Weeks and months of chipping away at his grief and his stoicism. All in the long-term plan. Now he's here, she's in pieces. The one day she needs to be alone. She should've cancelled, should've realised the time.

Jari looks around, looking for Kandi, who normally explodes at visitors as soon as they knock on the door. He takes off his coat and gently places it over an armchair, unsure what to do or say to Lotta. Uncomfortable at the sobs she's stifling.

"Are you OK?" he asks, knowing the answer is "no". His arms hang by his sides, useless.

Lotta straightens up. Her eyes sparkle in the low light. Her cheeks are wet. "They took her," she says. "Wolves. They killed Kandi."

"No. Please, no."

She nods as her face crumples. She tries to hide her tears, but her wracking shoulders and stilted breaths give her away. Jari steps forward, hooks an arm around her shoulders and pulls her into a wooden hug. She breathes in his scent – cut wood and earth. Practical but not unpleasant.

As he holds her close with one arm, she remembers that he's been there too. A year or so ago, when the pack came for his dog, Lori, one night. His fury and grief come back to her. Rage at the world for his dead wife coupled with the loss of the dog he'd reared by hand. The village whispers about his state of mind, about his drinking, about his unpredictability. They'd faded to nothing over time, but the imprint of his grief was still obvious in his bent shoulders and quiet words.

She didn't want to end up like that. Hating the world even for a brief period. She extricated herself from his awkward arm. Smiled up at him.

"Let's get that bottle open, shall we?"

***

Despite ruining the potatoes, the meat survived its time in the oven. Lotta, unable to move, stayed slumped on the sofa whilst Jari navigated her kitchen, returning with a plate of sliced meat and mustard for her. They ate in silence, the house quiet until the whisky came out.

"I couldn't find any ice in your freezer, so I used snow."

Jari leans forward to pass the whisky glass to Lotta, the last shape of the snow collapsing into the amber liquid as it melts. Her eyes remain fixed on the clock next to the television. His voice snaps her thoughts in two.

"Huh?"

"I used snow for the whisky." He forces a smile. "Hope that's OK."

"Sure." Without looking at the contents of the glass, she drains half of it. It burns the back of her throat, but she doesn't cough, just savours the fire that spreads through her.

Jari takes his place in the armchair opposite. He perches at the front of the seat, his back unsupported. Elbows on knees, he leans forward. Takes a sip of his drink. Watches Lotta watch the clock.

Minutes pass. The hands on the clock move round to seven o'clock. There's a beep from the alarm of the clock in another room. Lotta blinks. Sips the rest of her drink. Her limbs fold around herself, a blanket across her legs. A fire rages in the log burner. She watches it for a few seconds.

"It's time for the soaps," she says.

"Do you want me to put them on? I can always go if that's best ..."

"No. Don't go yet. Please." She drains her glass, puts it back on the table. "As soon as the theme music starts, every day, she'd come running from wherever she was to come and sit up here with me. Every damn day."

"That dog wasn't stupid. She had you under her thumb alright."

Lotta snorts, almost laughing, but tears still come. "She did. Dad would've said she was soft, but she wasn't. She never once let me down on a hunt. She was always there when it counted."

"Tell me how it happened."

"No."

"Lotta, you need to. Trust me. I've been where you are. I need to know."

"Why? Will it make you feel better?"

"No. Of course not."

"Why then?"

He finishes his own whisky, brings them both a refill, starts on the second before he speaks again.

"When they killed Lori, it was unfortunate, so most people said. Some probably said I was careless. Maybe I was, but the wolves never dared come close to the village before. We had no reason to take extra precautions then. When I found her – well, you probably heard about it all. I lost it." He smiles, head bowed towards his feet.

"You ran into the woods with two rifles and not wearing anything but your long johns. That's what I heard."

He doesn't look up. Instead, shakes his head. Sips his whisky, keeping his eyes from hers.

"Grief does funny things to you. Strange things. Losing Lori like that. Finding her like that. After what they'd done to her. All I wanted was revenge. All I wanted was blood."

"But you didn't get it?"

"They talked me round. Sammi. Steffen. Even Asko came home from Helsinki for a few days to stay with me. I was a wreck. Never sober. Spent my nights with my rifle, waiting by the door for them to come back. They didn't though. They'd got what they wanted and knew I had nothing else to give."

"Do you still wait by the door with a rifle every night?"

"No, but I should. They came back. Two nights ago. Digging and scratching around Hassa's kennel and post. Looking for her."

"No. The bastards."

"Two of them. By the time I got out there with the gun, they were too far away. I didn't want to go charging out into the dark on my own. I got the feeling, sounds stupid, but somehow that's what they wanted me to do. Make me make a mistake."

Lotta drains her second whisky, feels the burn subside into a craving for more. Her throat tingles at the thought. She straightens up on the sofa and pulls the blankets tightly around her, not caring how Jari sees her now. She suspects he's talking in a way he hasn't for years. Not since his wife passed.

"One waited in the woods until Kandi went out to play. I was inside, cooking. I had eyes on her. Then it appeared. Had her toy in its mouth. And she followed it into the forest." Her hands knit together beneath the blankets, her fingers aching under the pressure. "I went back for my rifle. Tracked them into the forest, but there were two sets of wolf tracks even though I'd only seen one. When I found them, they were staring into the trees, like they could see or hear something I couldn't. Then the wolf ..." She looks up at Jari, and he nods at her. "So I brought her back here, and I'm sure they were coming for me. Not to kill me maybe, but to scare me. Closing in."

Jari isn't looking at her now. He's sat back in the armchair, eyes on the ceiling. After a few seconds, he snaps forward. "Did you see the second wolf?"

"No. Not at all. Just the grey one."

He brushes hair back from his forehead. Shakes his head. "Me neither. I mean. I saw the two that came to the house, but when they ran away, I felt like there was another one close by. I didn't see it. Just had that feeling, you know?"

"Like when you're hunting, and you know there's prey nearby before you see it."

"Exactly."

Without being asked, he gets up and pours her another drink. The back door opens and closes with a clatter, then he reappears, glass extended towards her.

"I've been where you are now, Lotta. You know that. Everyone around here knows that. These animals, they aren't our colleagues or our pets. They're our family. In my case, Lori was all I had. Following Magda like that, it nearly broke me. I wasted a lot of time being angry and having too much self-pity. It nearly broke my business. All this stings now, but there'll be time to set it right. I promise."

She forces a smile, forces a nod. The only thing she hasn't forced this evening is the whisky down her throat. She feels as though she could drink for days. Drink the world dry. Until she fades to black and her body shuts down.

"They need to be stopped," she says. "Soon. They came for Hassa, they took Kandi. That would've been the two best hunting dogs in the village gone. They'd have wrecked our livelihoods."

She pauses, a hand goes to her mouth. "How will I hunt? Next season. Oh, Jesus. What am I going to do?"

Numbers and figures flash through her mind as she tries to calculate payments and bills and debts. Whisky has lubricated the wheels of her mind too much. The cogs slip, and the sums don't hold. A throbbing starts at her temple.

"You'll survive. It might not seem like it, but you will. There are options. There are always options. Trust me. This is the mistake I made. Overthought it all. Worried myself half into the grave about it. You've got help, just like I did. If needs be, me and Hassa will support your hunts. She's young, she can learn if she has to. We can make it work."

Lotta doesn't need to hear this right now, this kindness from Jari. At the start of the day, the thought of spending more time with him would've excited her, but all she can think about now is shutting herself away and planning how to kill every wolf this side of the Russian border.

"You won't have to wait long, you know, to get them."

More whisky finds its way into her system, boiling in the pit of her stomach. Jari leans forward.

"You need to know too. Deserve to know now." Jari takes a sip himself, sets the glass on the table. "Yesterday morning, after I saw the wolves, I tracked them. With Steffen and Asko. Wanted to see where they'd gone. People are worried. We needed to make sure our village is safe."

She nods her agreement.

"They'd chased off one of Sammi's elk. Another one. Chased the poor thing down for miles. Past my property, across Sammi's, out into the wider forest. When we found the scene, Christ. The wolves had torn it apart. They'd left nothing. It wasn't just a kill. They'd gone crazy, ripped the thing to shreds. All eight of them, feasting on it. They'd chased it down for fun. They didn't need to run it down that far."

"Why am I only hearing about this now?"

"We're going to call a meeting soon to discuss what should be done. To discuss culling them."

"What else are you waiting for, Jari? We should've already done this."

"We don't want to panic people. There are already families worried. We can't lose any more people from this village. There's barely enough of us as it is."

"Kandi could still be here if we'd acted sooner."

"I'm sorry, Lotta. I would've gone straight out after them, but it's not that easy, is it? Everyone needs to know, needs to be informed. Those who don't hunt might not want us to go charging out there because of a dog. They don't understand."

"But *you* do. *You know*. You should've rounded them up that morning. Instead, you sat on your hands and had a few beers whilst my dog got *murdered* out in those trees. In sight of my own fucking home."

"No. I want them gone. Nobody wants them gone more than me, but we can't just ride out like cowboys into the forest and mow them down."

"Says who?"

He picks up his drink and drains it. Shrugs. "Asko. Some others. Look, I think I've done everything I can here. I'm sorry about Kandi, truly I am. We'll sort this soon, I promise. Please keep this to yourself. We can't risk a panic. If that happens, it'll only get worse. Believe me."

"You've got a week to make a decision, or I'm calling every house in this village and telling them what you told me."

"We will sort it."

"One week."

"OK."

She gets to her feet, lets the blankets slip from her shoulders to the floor. One arm gestures out towards the door. "I think you'd better go."

"I'm sorry, Lotta. We're trying to do our best for the community."

"Please leave."

He gets up and puts on his coat, pulls his hat down over his already matted hair. By the door, he stops, slips on his snow boots. Looks over at her.

"We never meant to hurt anyone. We're trying to look after this village."

"You're not the fucking mayor, Jari. You're a fucking hunter. Start acting like one."

She strides past him and opens the door. Cold air races in, bringing flecks of snow with it. He walks past her into the darkness without a word. She slams the door behind him, turns the lock. Waits until she hears the engine of his truck fire up before she collapses to her knees in the hallway and lets her grief begin again in earnest.

Chapter Four

The trilling of his phone wakes Jari. There is no answerphone, so it rings out again and again into the darkness of his home. From her bed on the floor, Hassa stirs first. Her bark adds another layer of noise and insists he gets up.

He pads from the bedroom into the kitchen, where the phone cradle is screwed to the wall. He takes the handset down and tucks it under his chin as he slumps against the wall. Time is fluid in the darkness, but his body clock tells him that this is an antisocial hour.

"Hello?"

No answer.

"Hello?"

A sigh on the other end. The clank of glass on glass.

"Lotta?"

A cough and a chuckle in reply. "It's like that, is it?"

"Sammi? What the hell are you doing?"

"I'm drinking. Just like we used to. It's fun. You should try it again. Like the old days. Really go to town."

"It doesn't agree with me to drink that much. You know that."

"It agrees with me."

Jari sighs. Cold creeps across his shoulders, and he longs for rest, for a break.

"They're here again. The wolves."

"Now?"

"They woke me. Howling. Like they were calling to me. Telling me what they'd done."

"And what have they done?"

"Taken more from my herds. Four this time. Maybe more."

"Jesus Christ, Sammi."

"I'm sure I locked those gates. Certain. Or I was." There's a gulping sound down the line. A satisfied gasp. "But who can be sure of anything these days?"

"Oh, fuck. I'm sorry." Jari sinks down to his haunches, the phone cord stretching to its limit.

"So am I. Sorry that we didn't take your advice a few years back and put an end to those vermin when we had the chance. We should've done it then, Jari. Should've killed them all. I saw eight tonight. Maybe more. Some stayed in the light, some didn't. But even when I got the rifles out, they didn't panic."

"Did you hit any of them?"

"Not even close. They got out of range too quickly for me."

Jari pictures Sammi waking alone, squinting down his rifle and firing drunken pot-shots into the trees. Pictures his friend screaming into the darkness. He's not sure whether he can picture the wolves or not. Can't be sure if Sammi can be trusted after this many schnapps.

"What's the damage to your herd? Can you cope?"

"I'll assess it in the morning. Ring that fucking accountant of mine. Or the insurance. Maybe both."

"Perhaps lay off the schnapps before you do that, eh?"

"You some sort of fuckin' choir boy now you don't get drunk every night? I'm fine."

"I hope so."

"I'm fine."

"Call me tomorrow. Let me know the damage."

"Yes, sir."

"Don't act smart."

"I'll do it."

Sammi hangs up and leaves Jari sitting alone on his kitchen floor. He stares into the semi-darkness. The fire in his log burner is nothing but ash and futile embers. Its warmth barely stretches beyond the glass of the burner's door.

Jari pulls himself from the floor, puts the phone back in its cradle and collapses onto his bed. When Hassa jumps up to join him, he doesn't have the strength to push her away. Instead, he drapes an arm over her body, enjoying the heat of another being on the covers.

***

Sammi doesn't call and won't answer his phone.

Jari isn't rested and finds himself pacing his home after finishing his breakfast. He tries calling Sammi again, hoping that an engaged ringtone will at least show him that Sammi is up and taking care of business. The phone rings out, and Jari slams it down.

Hassa yips at his knees, desperate to be let out to exercise. This time cooped up in the house isn't good for either of them. The hyperactive dog is playing on Jari's last nerve, but after Lotta's story of the wolves' attack on Kandi, he isn't taking any chances. Instead, he shuts Hassa in the bathroom and snatches up his keys.

The drive to Sammi's farm is a slow one, even by the standards of local conditions. Each resident is responsible for the roads on their own land. An unwritten social contract demands they salt and clear the roads as best they can for the other residents. Sammi hasn't kept up his end of the bargain.

Sweat lingers under Jari's arms as he pulls the truck into the yard between Sammi's house and outbuildings. He doesn't dwell on the thought of navigating the winding path between the trees as he leaves. Promises himself that he'll refuse the inevitable drink Sammi will offer. He might not be a saint with the drink, but he's trying. Trying not to let Sammi drag him back into old ways and darker times.

Jari crunches his way to the front door and pounds it with a gloved fist. As he waits, he steps back, taking in the growing disrepair of the farmhouse. Portions of the wooden veneer have begun to rot. Sopping dark stains climb from the ground to shoulder height in some places. Higher up, a spool of insulation hangs out in the breeze, shimmering with moisture. Above the front door, one of the wooden windows is open a crack. He struggles to remember the layout of Sammi's house, whether the window is for his friend's bedroom or not. When Sammi entertains, he does it outside in the summer with barbecues and fires piled high with cooking meat. Jari has pissed in these woods more times than he cares to remember.

He knocks again. Shouts up at the open window. The only responses are the grunts of cattle from the outbuildings. Sammi never married, never had a serious partner from what Jari ever saw. If ever a place or a person needed a woman's touch or some extra care, it was Sammi's. As if Jari himself has any room to talk.

Shaking his head, Jari hammers the door again. He takes his glove off and smashes his bare hand against the wood, feeling the impact reverberate across his skin. He steps away from the door, pulling his glove back on. Inspects the darkened windows. Cups a hand against each of them. A living room littered with empty bottles, a kitchen in the same state. A dining room with a long table, one chair pulled out and left askew.

Back at the front door, Jari doesn't knock this time; he turns the handle and lets himself in. The house is silent, punctuated only by the ticking of a grandfather clock in the hallway. Shoes litter the hallway floor, snow boots and slippers left haphazardly.

No fire burns in the living room grate. Jari can't feel any difference between the temperature inside or out. He takes the stairs quickly, calling Sammi's name. Upstairs is a replica of downstairs, every room empty of Sammi and piled with junk. Sammi's bed is unmade. Sheets folded back and rippled across the bare mattress. A duvet and a fur blanket lie on the floor. By the open window, a rifle lies on its side, spent cartridges on the floor around it. An unopened box of ammunition on the dressing table nearby, an empty bottle of schnapps keeping it company.

Jari takes the stairs faster now. Jogging into the kitchen and letting himself out the back door. He pauses on the doorstep as an elk catches his eye from a few yards away. It stares at him, eye round and black, before it bolts past him across the open ground behind Sammi's house.

"What the fuck?"

As he nears the outbuilding, the rest of the herd pile out into the snow behind the first. Dozens of them, grunting and snorting, hooves pounding the snow as they blunder away from their home and out onto the frozen grassland that Sammi calls a garden. From there, they can dissipate into the forest.

Jari waits for them to pass, each weighing the same as car. It would be madness to try to intervene. Eventually, they are all gone. The doors of their home have been left swinging in the breeze, exposing the pens they lived in. The floor is hay and woodchip and mud. Reeks of shit and fur. Jari wanders into the outbuilding. Light arrows in through the gaps in the corrugated metal roofing.

He rounds the corner to the storage area at the back of the outbuilding, hidden behind the pens by a breezeblock wall.

He stops dead.

Sammi lies on his back in the far corner. Snow boots poke out from behind boxes of feed and chemicals. One of his legs is bent inwards at a strange angle, the foot pointing in a way it shouldn't.

Jari runs over and skids to a halt when he sees the state of his friend. A shotgun lies next to Sammi, one bare hand still clasped around the wooden stock.

Everything behind Sammi's face is gone. Splattered on the breezeblocks and the boxes behind him. Mingling with the mud and filth on the floor of the outbuilding.

Jari gags and turns away.

This is not his first time dealing with death, far from it, but this is a different experience from finding your father slumped over the yearly accounts, an empty bottle of pills in his hand and a half-spent bottle of whisky on the table. This is different to waking to find your wife cold and stiff next to you beneath the covers.

Those deaths weren't violent. Not like this. With its explosion of dark red and exposure of things that men aren't supposed to see.

He steps closer to Sammi, his composure regained. He's glad he is here alone to react to this scene in his own way, without the pressure to be brave or to put on a show. He takes a deep breath, holds the freezing air in his lungs until it burns, then slowly lets it go, feeling everything in him sag as his breath steams in front of his face.

He kneels. Steady again. Over the initial shock. Panic drops away from his senses and brings clarity to the details, to his own thoughts. Sammi died alone. He left nobody behind. No wife, no children, and no relatives that Jari has ever met. Whether Sammi was a good man or not isn't for Jari to judge, but his suicide will reverberate around the community. Incidents like this leave their mark.

There would always be a knock-on effect somewhere. Perhaps someone would scramble to buy the land and the farm, not that it would be worth much with its herds scattered to the forests. Perhaps someone from out of the area would try to make a go of the property. Both options are longshots. Outsiders don't move here often. This isn't a city with jobs and networks and connections.

Anyone who moves here looking to make money is either too desperate to think straight or too stupid to do their research.

The other knock-on effect is people fleeing. That slow drip-drip of people leaving the village gathers pace after incidents like this. As though it takes only one person to shake the others from their torpor. One tragedy to wake people up to the fact that they themselves are unhappy.

The kids always leave first. Be it for university or employment or just for adventure. Most don't return. Jari wonders who will be next to leave. It all comes down to money. Few people have the means to escape, even if they have the will. His money is on Helenka, with her two boys and absent husband. Every time he sees her, she's slumped, bent by what she carries. If she has the means, she'll go. He thinks of the others and of their own individual plights. There are no secrets in this place. Not really.

He shakes his head, still crouched over Sammi's corpse. He won't be leaving this place until it's his turn to ride out of it in a box. Some things are too entrenched. Outside of hunting and outside of this village, he has nothing. He is nothing.

Jari touches Sammi's hand lying flat on the ground, fingers curled and bent. There's some warmth to Sammi's skin, but it fades beneath Jari's fingers the longer he stays there.

After a few minutes of silence, Jari pulls himself up, ready to leave and to make the necessary calls. He scans the area, looking for anything he's missed.

On the sink at the back of the outbuilding, a faded envelope sits between the taps. The envelope is unaddressed. Missing a subject. Jari picks it up, his fingers raw and pink. Inside is a crumpled note, written in Sammi's bent handwriting. Jari squints at it.

I don't know who will find me and whoever it is, I'm sorry for the state of things.

There isn't much to say. This is down to money. Everything always is. The farm is hundreds of thousands of euros in debt. There's no end in sight for this. The noose is tight already. The time will come when I'm forced to leave, and there'll be nowhere to go. At least this way, I can pay the bastards back in kind. There's no wife or kids or other family to come to for the debt. It all dies with me.

This village has taken my soul. I could never afford to leave. The long nights on my own and the lack of any options, they've all added up. It's this or I drink myself to death in the snow after the bank kick me out.

The wolves are the last straw. The elk ... no matter what I do, they still take them. Night after night. Grinding me down. Chipping away at the herd. Howling all night. It's too much.

Jari stares at Sammi's body as he slots the note back into the envelope. Alone in the outbuilding, he shivers, already composing a note of his own in his head. Not that he's planning on going the same way as Sammi, but one day, there'll be a need. He'll have to communicate his final thoughts to whoever finds him when it's all said and done. That he'll die alone is not in any doubt. Even if someone would have him, he's no appetite to remarry after Magda. Lotta seemed an option for companionship for a while, but he knows that window has slammed shut following Kandi's death and her subsequent fury. The thought leaves him indifferent.

He pockets the note and leaves the outbuilding. Above the impenetrable line of trees, the sun is attempting to rise. Instead of the deep concrete grey, the sky is now polished steel. The brightest day he can remember for weeks.

A few elk are still visible along the treeline, where the forest grows exhausted and gives way to a clearing of grassland. They jump and trot, as though celebrating their newfound freedom. Jari watches them, hand cupped above his eyes. His mind isn't on them; he's already written off their survival. The majority have been reared in captivity, and they'll lack the skills to cope for a whole winter in the wild.

Instead, his mind is on the barbecues and parties Sammi has hosted here over the years. The beers passed around freely. Hunks of elk meat cooking over flames. Sausages sizzling. A table of desserts brought by the attendees left out to be shared by everyone. Music blasting out, old Springsteen songs and eighties rock.

Those times are gone now. They'd passed even before this happened. The signs were all there: Sammi withdrawing more and more. Jari bites his lip, trying to stop calling himself selfish for not checking on his friend enough.

There are calls to be made. He swings the outbuilding doors shut and pulls the bar into place, sealing Sammi inside. He walks back to his truck, crunching over the snow, lost in thoughts of his own and wondering who he needs to speak to first.

Chapter Five

From his front window, he sees the coroner's van pass on the winding road down to Sammi's house. Over the phone, they asked him to go with them and show them the body. He declined. He's seen enough for one day. Has no stomach to set eyes on Sammi again.

A plate of half-eaten bacon and eggs congeals on the table in front of him. It's a waste that he already regrets. His stores are running low, and the thought of obtaining more food seems too monumental to deal with right now.

From outside, Hassa whines and howls. He's tethered her up so she can run around and shit, leaving him in peace on the sofa. He shuts the curtains, having no need for the daylight or the outside world.

He turns on the TV. It's on a news channel. He watches it for a moment, unsure of the issue they're discussing. It only adds to his feeling that the outside world is more trouble than it's worth some days. Instead, he flicks the DVD player on. It loads up with the BBC logo and the cheesy intro music to Magda's favourite sitcom. He clicks "play", and the familiar faces of the actors appear. Faces as familiar as his own. Faces he's watched every night for months on end.

He checks the time. Barely afternoon. Already darkness is starting to close off the world. Tightening like a hand closing slowly around the world. He pictures Sammi's hand, turned upwards in the outbuilding. The coroners will be there soon. Taking photographs and moving Sammi up onto the gurney, into the back of their van.

He sighs. His mind screams for entertainment. He licks his lips. Enjoys the scrape of the stubble around his mouth as he brushes it with his tongue. It took a long time to get his drinking under control after Magda and then again after Lori. He didn't do it alone. Sammi helped him where he could before he succumbed to his own demons. Steffen too. When Asko returned from Helsinki, he chipped in. Since then, he's always worked to a mantra of moderation that starts with one simple rule.

Don't drink in the daytime.

He checks his watch again. Seven minutes past twelve. There are hours to go.

The canned laughter from the television grates on him. His fingers twitch, and for want of something to do, he rolls and lights a cigarette despite the feeble rations of tobacco he has left. He pulls the smoke in deep and tries to pretend it doesn't matter.

After a few minutes, he gets up and puts some coffee on. It's cheap and poor quality, but it goes well with his cigarette. When it's ready, he pours a cup and stands back in front of his sofa, staring up at the picture of Magda on the mantelpiece and praying to his dead wife for the strength to last until the darkness.

***

Sometime after eight, the phone rings. The TV plays the same endless loop of DVD menu as Jari slumps on the couch, his eyes on the ceiling and the walls around him. The ringing drags him from his vigil. His thoughts are not even clear to himself. Another sound punctuates the regular bleating of the phone, high-pitched and erratic. He sits up straight, snapped to attention now.

Hassa.

He's on his feet. Blankets that he can't remember getting from the bedroom tumble to the floor, knocking over his half-full coffee cup. At the door, he wrestles on his boots, the phone constantly nagging for his attention.

"Fuck off!" he shouts as he pulls the second boot on and jerks the door open.

Outside, the cold snatches his breath, remorseless in its actions. Breezes tousle his hair, mocking him. The yellow glow from the porch light blinds him, reducing his vision to only a few square feet. Behind the glare, the forest looms, a wall of black.

On the front lawn, Hassa crouches in the snow, claws out, teeth bared. She's growling, ears pinned back. Her form is sleek and sharp. Jari calls down to her, trying to snap her away from whatever she's doing. He's never seen her like this before.

"Hassa! Hassa!" He clicks his fingers, the call she usually responds to. No reply. With the air this cold, he won't be able to click for much longer before numbness steals his mobility.

In the snow, the dog still growls. He puts a hand above his eyes, straining to see movement in the dark of the forest. There's nothing. Just the harsh noises from Hassa's throat.

Jari cannot move from the top step of his porch. Hassa is tethered to her post in the yard, tied up like meat to be fed to a predator. The gun dog's hackles raise even further. Her whole body is distorted beyond its usual shape. The adrenaline in her veins gives her an almost demonic quality in the unnatural light.

There's something out there. Out of sight in the darkness, a predator. Jari knows it's a wolf. Or wolves. But not being able to see them somehow gives the animals a mystique he's never experienced before. Blood thumps through his temples and throat, so hard he imagines Hassa can hear it.

Hassa yowls, all teeth and terror.

He needs to get down there, untie her and bring her inside. She's barely ten yards away from him, but his feet are too heavy, and his muscles have surrendered their strength.

Another sound, from beyond the circle of the porch light, rustling in the foliage. Again, he squints into the darkness, desperate for physical evidence of the sound if only to convince himself that it is real. All there is to see is the endless black of the forest.

The same sound again. Deliberate. Wolves can move as silently as they need to when stalking their prey. If they're heard, it's because they want to be heard.

He takes a breath.

Jari jumps down from the porch into the snow below. He sinks up to his knees, and the cold up his calves shocks the rest of his brain into life. He wades through the powder to Hassa. The dog doesn't look at him as he fumbles with the leash. Numb hands fumble with the knot.

It won't give.

He turns his head back to the front door, considering going in for a knife to cut Hassa free, but he knows what he'll find if he leaves her alone for another minute more. Somehow, he's dimly aware that beyond all this, the phone is still ringing inside the house. The sound mocks him through the open door, a reminder that the cold is invading his home.

"Come on!" he yells into the sky above him.

After pulling at the knot, his fingers gain purchase, and he unravels the leash. Sensing give, Hassa darts forward. Jari digs his heels into the snow and pulls against her. Hassa yowls as her collar digs into her throat. Straining, Jari reels her in, pulling the leash towards himself hand over fist until the dog is close enough that he can scoop her up into his arms. She sinks her teeth into his forearm, and he almost drops her in surprise. He holds her tighter and staggers up the stairs, his bodyweight on the handrail as he thuds inside and slams the door shut.

As soon as Hassa's feet touch the floor, she turns to the door, barking and growling, hurling herself against it whilst Jari slots the locks shut. Hassa tries four times to get back outside, smashing her head against the wood of the door before giving up, panting. Dark eyes train on Jari, pink tongue lolling past her jaw.

Despite the throbbing in his forearm, he kicks off his boots and kneels in front of her, hand out. Hassa nuzzles his hand, licks the skin. A canine apology. As his heartbeat returns to normal, he strokes the back of her head, the spot she likes best. Sweat patches sting in the chill under his arms and down his back.

He rolls up his sleeve, scowling at the punctures in the cloth. Blood shines in the light of the living room from the four wounds in his arm. They aren't deep. Ignoring the still ringing phone, he washes the cuts and wraps them in gauze from the first aid kit under the sink. Breathless, he snatches up the bottle of schnapps on the counter and swigs back a couple of mouthfuls. Feels his breathing calm at the burn in his throat.

Unable to take it anymore, he snatches up the receiver of the phone. "What? What the fuck do you want?"

A familiar voice. "Jari. Where have you been?"

"Long story, Asko. What's so important?"

"Two families have gone. Disappeared. Heikkinens out by the lake. Looks like they left a while ago. I've just seen the Lehtonens go past. Both trucks loaded up. Trailers on them both. They're done."

Jari doesn't know what to say. He leans against the wall, phone still cupped to his ear.

"We need to decide what to do. If we're going to save this community, we have to make decisions."

"Is that what you want, Asko? To save this community? Are you sure you won't be next? Heading back to Helsinki when things get tough."

"What are you talking about? Pia and me, we came back to start a new life here. To help the place thrive. We want to raise children here."

Jari laughs. "Here? Where your kids would get bussed to school miles away? What is there here?"

"Hunting. Fishing. Nature. A proper way to live, Jari. This place is worth saving."

"I don't know anymore."

"Bullshit. You're of this village. If you don't think it's worth saving, then nobody will."

Jari doesn't reply.

A sigh down the phone. "All I'm saying is, people around here will listen to you. Whatever you want to do. If you think this place is worth something, then you need to say something pretty quickly. They won't rally around me, not after I spent some time away. But you, you can make a difference."

"I thought you didn't want to cull the wolves?"

"I never said anything about culling them. I'm talking about saving the village, taking steps to let everyone coexist."

"We can't fucking coexist, Asko. Jesus Christ, man. You've watched a family leave with your own eyes. I've found Sammi dead today with his head fucking blown off. That's down to the wolves."

Asko remains silent.

"I'll stand up for this place, but I'm not standing up for the wolves because they're the problem here. Nobody else. I've just about managed to save Hassa tonight from them. This is no way to live already, and it's only going to get worse."

"Jari, we can make this work. I promise you. There's no need to cull them."

"We should've done it a long time ago, and nothing you say can change my mind. I'm going to call the villagers together this week, and we'll take it to a vote. You will get your chance to speak, same as everyone else, but whatever the majority decides is what we're going to do."

"I'll be there. I'll speak up. I'm not afraid to be the voice of common sense. Maybe all it'll take is a reasoned plan to look after the village."

"Maybe. But there are people like me, baying for blood. Prepare yourself for that. Me and Lotta, we've lost animals, basically family members. Steffen will be devastated by Sammi's death. You've got people with kids who are scared to let them out after dark. People are frightened, Asko. People are angry. Don't underestimate that."

"I understand it all, Jari. But tell me this: if *you* get outvoted, what will you do? Promise me you'll honour whatever is decided. There's no point voting if you're going to go into the forest alone like Rambo on some deranged killing spree."

"It doesn't sound like you trust me."

"I trust you with my life, but I want your word."

"You've got my word. The only thing I want from you is a guarantee that you'll be there when the cull starts and that you'll participate. We will need all the decent marksmen we can get, especially now we've lost two decent hunters in recent weeks."

"As if I need to say it, but of course."

"Good. I'll call the vote for tomorrow night."

Jari hangs up the phone, his t-shirt further drenched in sweat. Without thinking, he scratches at the bandage on his arm, looks down at spots of blood soaked into the thin material. He bites his lip and pours himself a decent measure of schnapps into a tumbler.

Chapter Six

Beneath the rumble and clink of chained tyres over compacted snow and ice, the radio grumbles for attention. Hands tight on the steering wheel, Helenka listens in, straining over the noise of the car and from the backseat. A monotone newscaster talks about job losses in Helsinki and problems with the European Union. Rich people problems. She shakes her head and turns off the radio. The truck doesn't get any quieter.

Behind her, on the backseat of the truck's cab, Mikael and Olaf wrestle each other. Seatbelts dangle behind them, discarded and useless. Mikael shoves Olaf's face against the glass of the window, holding him at arm's length and putting his weight behind it. After a moment of grunting, Olaf starts to laugh and wrenches himself out of the hold, twisting Mikael's arm up behind his back. Mikael now grunts, trying not to show pain.

"Bastard," he calls out.

"Shitbag," Olaf laughs.

"Knock it off, now." The truck slips on gathered snow, and Helenka corrects its course without thinking, eyes darkened in annoyance reflecting in the rear-view mirror.

On the dashboard, the amber digits of the clock tell her the window is closing. Disbelieving what she's seen, she checks her watch, puts her foot down, feels the back end slide out and corrects again.

"Nice driving, Mum," Mikael shouts as his brother topples into him.

"It's like she's getting worse at it on purpose," Olaf says.

"Or she's so old she's forgetting how to do it."

Ignoring her sons, she mashes her foot to the floor. Her mind is everywhere but on the road. She calculates whether it's worth trying to get to Steffen's this morning or not. Maria will have already left for work, but by the time Helenka's got the boys to the bus stop, she'll be out of time to get to Steffen and back in time for work.

She wants to scream at the two idiots in the backseat. Shout in their faces for messing around all morning, for not eating quickly enough, for not getting dressed when she asked them. Most of all, she wants to scream at them to stop looking and sounding like their piece of shit father. But that isn't fair. That part they can't control.

Part of her just wants something for herself. Someone to make her feel special for an hour. Even if it's someone else's husband. Surely, after years of wrangling the two boys night and day, she deserves that. Deserves some affection and attention. Deserves to be seen by someone else as an adult, as a woman.

Skidding, the truck broadsides round the corner. Behind her, the boys mock-scream, hands on faces like Macaulay Culkin in *Home Alone*. But as the truck straightens, they click their seatbelts on.

It isn't Helenka's turn to wait at the bus stop today, to oversee the rabble of local kids being bussed off to the school. Inari will be there, with her perfect hair and cherubic kids. She'll keep watch over the lot of them. The idea itself is laughable – that an unarmed parent is any deterrent for the wolves – but as it isn't her turn, she can still make it to see Steffen. Her chest constricts at the thought of opening his front door and tumbling into his bed. She takes a deep breath, steadies herself.

Makes a decision.

Battling the steering wheel, she brings the truck to a skidding stop by the side of the road. Snow is piled high next to them, ploughed drifts frozen in the night.

"Holy shit, Mum. You nearly broke my neck," Olaf says. Mikael titters along with his older brother's cursing.

"What have I told you about swearing in front of me?" She doesn't turn around. She watches in the rear-view mirror.

"Shit. Must've forgotten." They both scoff and giggle like a pair of jackals.

"Get out. Now. Behave yourselves at school for once. I will not come and see that headteacher again." Her voice is a low growl she doesn't recognise.

Olaf looks to Mikael, the pair wearing near-identical smirks. Helenka struggles to find the logic for having two children so close together, but that part of her brain is long since closed.

"Do you think we should, Mikki?"

"Absolutely not, O. Drive on, Mummy. Drive on." Mikael claps his hands like a Prime Minister ordering his stooges.

"I tell you what, Mikki. I don't think Dad would treat us like this, would he?"

"Absolutely not. He'd have the red carpet out for us, like we deserve."

Helenka whips round in her seat, jaw set. "Well, your father isn't here, is he? He's off in the city with some young bitch." She covers her mouth, but the words have already tumbled out.

"He had the right idea. It's boring around here. Total shithole," Mikael says.

Tears come to her eyes, threatening to smudge the makeup she has so carefully applied. "I'm doing my best for you both. That's all I've ever done."

At the sight of her tears, the boys fold their hands and fix their eyes downwards.

"We didn't mean you, Mum. It's just this place. It's boring. There's nothing to do," Olaf says.

"There's no football team. I can't even get my Xbox online," Mikael says, a whine to his voice making him sound younger than his fourteen years.

"We've always lived here, boys. This isn't my fault. This is the only home you've ever known. Your dad grew up here."

"Well, he isn't living here anymore, is he? What's keeping us?"

"You know what. We can't afford to move."

"Dad would send us money. He's got a nice place over in Tampere."

"I'm not asking your father for money. End of discussion."

"You should think about it," Olaf says. "Tampere is great. There's so much going on."

"Your father is hundreds of miles away, and that's fine by me. I'd make it even further if I could."

The boys continue to chatter in the backseat, but Helenka isn't even half listening. She scans the road ahead for any signs of Inari. They're alone on the road. There's nobody else in sight. Her phone buzzes in her pocket, and she reads the message.

Inari: *Markus is off today. Can't do bus stop duty. Sorry. X*

Not now. She clenches her hands so tightly she wonders if she could break the phone in two. She needs this, needs the comfort of Steffen's arms.

"Get out."

"What?" Mikael says. "I thought you were joking?"

"Who's the chaperone?" Olaf pipes up.

"Get out," Helenka says again. The boys look at each other. "Get out, get out, get out!" Her voice rises in pitch and volume the more she repeats the words. Wheeling round in her seat, she shoos the boys, herding them towards the door and out into the snow. They scrabble, grabbing bags and hats. Complaining, but the words mean nothing to her. Olaf opens his door, and they both tumble out onto the frozen road.

With the door still open, Olaf looks up at his mother. "What about the chaperone? We'll be on our own."

"The daylight's increasing. You can see fine. I need to go. I'll be late for work."

"But it's early still."

"Just shut up and shut the door."

For once, Olaf does what he's told, and Helenka floors the accelerator. Chained tyres spin and grasp purchase on the compacted snow. The truck shoots forward and straightens out on the road as Helenka powers towards Steffen's place.

***

Alone in the snow, the boys exchange a glance. Although they've noticed their mother become more distracted over the last couple of months, this is something new. They watch the truck disappear in silence, breath clouding in front of them. Mikael adjusts his hat and turns to his brother.

"She's finally lost the plot."

"Second child syndrome, Mikki. She's gone mad having to stare at your ugly face all day."

"Get fucked." Mikael shoves his brother and laughs as Olaf's momentum makes him stagger into the packed snow at the side of the road.

"It's true though, she's never been the same since you came along."

"As if you can even remember life without me. She's gone mad since Dad left."

"Feels like we all have."

They walk in the middle of the road towards the bus stop. Piled snow at the side of them creates banks higher than their heads. Beyond the drifts, pines crusted with snow tower over everything. Shining white sentinels against the steely sky.

"Did you mean what you said about moving away?" Olaf asks.

"Yeah, pretty much. I shouldn't have said we like the city more. I didn't mean to upset Mum, but it's better there. There's nothing here, is there? Just hunting and trapping. Bit of fishing. Boring. Like I said."

"You could be a farmer."

"I just said hunting was boring, pretty sure farming is worse. Do you not want to leave?"

"I've thought about it. I don't know. What about Mum?"

"What about her? She could come too."

"Well, you definitely need to leave the village. If you don't, you'll end up marrying Salli Forssell. I've seen her staring at you in school. She wants you badly."

Mikael flushes. Shoves his brother again. Tries to dish out a dead arm, but Olaf's layers cushion the blow.

"Fuck off, *junior*," Olaf says.

"I am not marrying Salli fucking Forssell."

"Well, not with that attitude."

"Son of a bitch. Stop that now, or I'll break your face."

"Break my face? You can barely reach it."

Mikael turns to face his brother. The year between them equates now to less than a centimetre in height. Mikael smiles then meets his brother's eye. Olaf isn't smiling, isn't ready for a quick wrestle before school. Olaf's head is cocked to one side, his eyes on the trees behind.

Mikael shoves his brother, not in the mood for school but ready to release some frustration with a quick scrap. "Come on, you pussy, hit me. Mum can't see. Shame nobody else will see when I kick your ass."

"Shut up."

Mikael pushes Olaf again, but Olaf isn't paying attention.

"Shut up," Olaf repeats. "Seriously."

Mikael lowers his voice, falling in with what his brother wants. "What's going on?"

"Listen."

"I can't hear anything."

"Exactly. No birds. No animals. No cars. Nothing."

"So what?"

"There's a reason for that. Come on." Olaf grabs his brother's arm and drags him over the packed snow into the concrete hut that acts as a bus shelter. The jutting concrete's right angles are the antithesis of the nature running wild around it.

Inside the shelter, the boys crouch beneath the low roof. Olaf's teeth clack. He doesn't tell his brother that it isn't just down to the cold.

"Mikki. Keep quiet and don't move."

"O, what the fuck is going on?"

"There's a wolf in the road."

"No, there isn't."

"Mikki, look at me. Am I fucking around?"

Mikael meets his brother's widening eyes, reads his emotions as easily as understanding his own. Shakes his head. "No. You're not."

"It must've seen us or smelled us or whatever they do. If I saw it, it definitely saw me."

"Holy shit. What are we going to do?"

"Let's have a look, see if we can see it. It might have gone off. They don't like the daytime. Maybe? Or is it the nighttime?" Olaf puts his hands to the side of his face. Eyes wild.

"No idea. Come on."

Discarding their backpacks into the inches of snow gathered inside the shelter, the two boys crawl on their knees to the opening. Signalling to his brother, Olaf pokes his head around the side of the shelter's gaping entrance, aware of the lack of a door and the scant protection it might've offered.

The wolf stands in the middle of the road, nose to floor, breath forming around it. Its sleek, grey frame is a dirty contrast to the morning snow around it. Olaf watches the wolf raise its head. Brilliant yellow eyes fixed on his. Olaf shoots back inside the hut. The tears in his eyes tell Mikael everything he needs to know.

"We need to do something," Olaf says. "It knows we're here."

Together they scour through the snow gathered inside the shelter, searching for a discarded stick or something sharp. The adolescent inside Mikael hopes to find a discarded shotgun. But they come up with nothing. Their schoolbags produce similar results: flasks and textbooks offering little hope. Even their phones don't help, by the time someone arrives, they'll be meat.

The boys are panting by the time they've finished their search. Sweat beads down from beneath their hats, their fingers clammy inside their gloves.

"Why did Mum leave us here?" Mikael's voice borders on a whimper.

Olaf shakes his head. "What if we don't see her again? What if the bus doesn't come?"

"Shut up." Mikael takes charge now. Movement in the trees catches his eye. He holds up a palm to his brother, silencing him. Both boys turn to the trees outside the shelter. Mikael points. Dark shapes flit between the trees. Their movements are slick and purposeful. Five wolves move in a wide circle around the shelter, crossing the road as they narrow the circle down. Each of them is a shade of grey, the colour of ash and metal. They move with a lolling gait, almost trotting, taking their time to narrow the gap between themselves and the shelter. They communicate in a series of barks, teeth snapping at each other.

"Holy shit, holy shit, holy shit ..."

"Shut up."

"There's a whole pack of them out there."

"Doesn't make any difference, Mik. We can't defend ourselves against one of them, let alone a pack." Olaf keeps his face turned towards the road as he speaks. "Look at how they're moving, you see it?"

"See what?"

"We studied this in biology. They're closing the gap. They're hunting us. This isn't an accident. They're meant to be here."

"What are we going to do?" Mikki doesn't flinch as tears roll down his cheeks. All semblance of bravado has gone. He looks at his brother. Olaf's face is grey, like a man on his deathbed. "We can't fight them. We've got nothing."

Cold settles deep inside Olaf's bones. His throat is tight around the freezing air he breathes. "We've got to run for it. Down the road. Steffen's place isn't far from here. If him and Maria are home, they've got guns. They could save us."

"Just follow the road?"

"Yeah. And don't look back."

Mikael gets to his feet, stooped below the low roof of the shelter. He pulls his brother to his feet. "You ready, O?"

Olaf nods, breath freezing around him. He looks out of the shelter. The wolf in the road is still there, eyes fixed on the hut. It stands so still it could be a statue. A horrible joke.

Olaf wonders how fast the wolf will close the gap. They've got a good head start, but it won't last. Can't last. He wonders how sharp the wolves' teeth are. What it will feel like for those teeth to pierce his flesh.

He wonders which of the brothers will die first.

Says a silent prayer that he won't have to watch Mikael be torn to pieces.

"OK," he whispers. "On three, we sprint. No looking back. If I fall, don't stop. Just keep going. Save yourself."

"But."

"Do it."

Mikael nods. The boys stand shoulder to shoulder just inside the hut, bent like sprinters under starter's orders.

Olaf counts silently using his fingers.

One. Two. Three.

They burst out of the shelter, away from their pathetic sanctuary. Scramble over the ploughed drifts and onto the firmer surface of the road. Heads down, they sprint as best they can. Every third step slides on the slick surface. There's the hiss of their jackets as they power forward, their rucksacks shaking from side to side.

Gravel and black ice litter the road in haphazard patterns, alternately shimmering and dull under the growing morning light. Mikael slips, and Olaf drags him by his backpack into an upright position, barely breaking stride.

Behind them, the wolf on the road barks – a brutal sound that echoes from the banks around them. Five corresponding barks. There's a scrabble of claws on the road surface. Staccato at first as the wolf struggles for purchase, but then it gathers pace. A constant rhythm.

Olaf sees his brother's face in his peripheral vision. Puce and panting. Knows his own is the same. He stays focused on the road and keeping each step as secure as it can be. He ignores the dark shapes on the banks above them. Their panting and their calls. The sense that they are enjoying the chase even more than they will enjoy the inevitable kill.

"Oh, fuck. They're getting closer." Mikael pants.

"Keep. Going."

Every step is one closer to escape, to survival. A single slip will lead to pain and worse. Exertion weighs on them both. Their breaths are ragged, their running form lost. Arms and legs are wild and uncoordinated. Stitches digging into their sides, cutting into their breathing.

Barking and snarling comes from all around them, getting closer, louder. The air is full of the sounds of hunger, of agitation and of bloodlust.

Each boy's breathing echoes the other's. Olaf pushes as hard as he can, aware that he's slowing down. A deep burn in his calves. Part of him ponders stopping, taking the hit for his brother, letting him get on and live his life away from this terrifying village. There's no way they can make it to Steffen's. They likely won't last another half-mile.

It isn't fair to take them both.

His thoughts are interrupted by the rattle of chains and the whoosh of hydraulics. There's a crunch of gears as the top of the bus appears over the crest of the rise ahead. Mikael whoops and shouts, wasting breath as he does so. Around them, the wolves burst into life again, calling to each other with more urgency and aggression. Neither boy dares look anywhere but at the oncoming yellow bus.

They race towards the bus, neither daring to look back. Olaf imagines a wolf's teeth inches from the soft meat of his calves, yellow teeth poised. Mikael keeps his head down, bent forwards, eyes on the bus.

Ahead, the bus grinds to a half. Its emissions fill the air with vapour and the choking scent of petrol. The throaty roar of the engine dominates their hearing, as though chugging through their minds. Behind the dirt-speckled windscreen, the driver watches them sprint.

With the grating of plastic and metal, the door slides open. The boys come to a skidding halt, almost overshooting the entrance before scrambling up the stairs to the driver. They bend double, panting and sweating. Mikael grabs the driver's arm.

"Get that door shut now."

The driver shakes his arm loose, presses the button, and the doors thud shut. "Don't you dare touch me. Where are the others?"

"It's just us today."

"Don't lie to me."

"It is."

"Did you see the wolves? We have to get going. Now!"

The driver squints, scans the road ahead, then sucks his teeth and shakes his head. "You've been watching too many films, boys. Sit down."

"But the wolves. Seriously. They were here."

The driver slams the bus into gear. The floor jolts at the crunch of the gearbox. "Sit down," he barks over his shoulder as the bus pulls away.

The boys stumble along the aisle, taking seats at the back of the empty bus. They rip at their coats and hats, exposing the clammy skin beneath. They bask in the relative warmth of the vehicle.

"What the fuck was that?" Olaf says as he slumps next to his brother.

Mikael stares out the window, watching the brilliant white embankments stream past. There are no wolves. The wide eyes of his brother staring back at him are the only evidence they were ever there at all.

Chapter Seven

Jari can't remember volunteering to host the meeting, but here they are. There are a few villagers missing, men with young children have left their wives at home, but those are the exceptions. There's a representative of every household in the village here bar one, yet his house doesn't seem full. Empty spaces in the corners glare at him. The spectres of Magda and Sammi and the families and children who have escaped to better things.

At least in their opinion.

As if to counter the desolation of the unoccupied spaces, one of Jari's nearest neighbours, Inari, stands in the centre of the room, rocking her small baby. The child coos and babbles as Lotta leans over him and waggles her fingers. Jari and Lotta have avoided eye contact and standing near each other. In a house the size of Jari's, it takes some coordination. For months, their growing friendship was the talk of the village. The committed singleton and the tragically bereaved hunter. Even though Jari himself never knew his own intentions towards Lotta, to be talked about for something other than being widowed gave him a sense of being alive he hadn't felt in years.

Now, as he stood watching her out of the side of his eye, he wanted nothing more than for her and everyone else to be gone. Heat crept up his cheeks. He'd felt foolish leaving Lotta's house that night, but worse still, he'd felt stupid because he couldn't figure out exactly what he was supposed to have done wrong.

Steffen hands him a beer, and he sucks it down, the cool lager an antidote to the growing stuffiness of the house. In a lull in the chatter, he takes off his thick, woollen jumper and reddens further when Steffen wolf whistles. "Fuck you," he says to his friend, getting nothing but a snigger in return.

Tommi leans inside the fridge, only his legs visible as he scrambles around. He pulls himself out, arms loaded with cans of beer that he passes to anyone within touching distance. Tommi stumbles back towards the armchair he's occupied since he arrived. He lurches and knocks the TV stand. The flatscreen wobbles dangerously, the reflection of the room in its black face distorting with the movement. Tommi collapses into the chair and slops his open beer down his front. Those around him laugh, and Tommi slurps down his can as though he lives here. Jari curls and uncurls his fingers. Tommi's never been good for anything other than getting drunk, but then people in glasshouses ... He puts his own beer on the mantelpiece, its contents now soured on his tongue.

Jari and Steffen are wedged at the front of the room, packed in front of the log burner. It's as though Jari is being cooked. His trousers are hot to the touch, and his skin is gently roasting beneath them.

There's a lull in the conversation as Tommi finishes telling his joke.

"And then he gets home from the hunt, and the elk's fucking his wife!"

Those around Tommi burst into laughter but immediately stifle it as they see the faces of Lotta, Jari and Steffen. They take sips of their drinks and bow their heads. Silence grows over the room until it's punctured by Asko and Pia opening the front door. Muttered complaints follow about getting the door shut and the heat getting out. The couple dust snow from their coats, their faces pink from the chill. Everyone turns away to give them time to take off their outdoor clothes.

Asko and Pia integrate themselves with the crowd, mingling and exchanging quips. Someone passes them both a beer, but they refuse, stick to Diet Coke instead. Jari watches all this. His face knitted into an unconscious frown. He can't remember the last time Asko turned down a beer, but then he can't remember when he and Asko disagreed over something so important.

He struggles to recall any time he's spent alone with Asko since his friend has returned from Helsinki. Things change, he understands that. Acknowledges that perhaps he hasn't been the easiest person to approach since Magda's death. But still. It's an easy matter to solve. He decides to make a point of inviting Asko over for a beer one night. Making that plan they've been meaning to make for months. Some company will do Jari good. Perhaps some space from home will do Asko good too. Who knows?

The backslapping and chatter bubbles up again after the silence over Tommi's punchline. Asko nods to Jari through the crowd, tips his can of Coke in Jari's direction. Pia puts her hands on Asko's arm and whispers something to him. Asko nods without taking his eyes from Jari.

"Enough!"

The conversations die instantly. Everyone's eyes follow the sound. Lotta stands in the middle of the room. Inari shrinks back from her, baby beginning to wriggle in her arms.

"Enough. We've been here long enough, even though some people only bother showing up when it suits them."

She turns to Asko and Pia, who both stare at the floor. Jari hides his smile behind his can of beer.

"We're here to talk. We're here to make a decision tonight. This is why."

She bends down and picks up the holdall at her feet. Balances it on top of the nearest armchair.

"Don't," Jari mutters, but she either doesn't listen or doesn't hear.

Lotta unzips the bag, and the stench that's been haunting the house pours out immediately. Those nearest to her recoil. Helenka steps back, pulling her two gangly boys with her, her arms reaching up to wrap around each of their shoulders.

Lotta pulls the bag open wider, tipping it and showing it around the room. Tommi stifles a laugh and pretends to cough. Others look and then look away. Inside the bag is Kandi's corpse. Her head is still twisted at the same hideous angle the wolves left it at. Her teeth are exposed by shrinking, decaying skin.

"This is why we're here. Because these *monsters* are doing what they want in our village. Murdering our pets. Robbing us of our companions." Tears trickle down her face, around the lines near her mouth. She gasps and rubs at them, shaking her head. "These *bastards* need stopping. This has gone too far."

Silence greets her words. She hangs her head over the bag with Kandi's corpse inside, stares at her dead pet and sobs openly, shoulders heaving. Nobody moves to comfort her. They all stare at their drinks or the floor.

Jari takes a sip of lager. Clears his throat. Steps as far from the log burner as he can before he speaks.

"I've been where Lotta is now. Lori died in similar circumstances." He avoids looking directly at anyone as he speaks. He doesn't fancy the violence this might lead to. "Some of you said it was my own fault. That I left Lori outside like a piece of meat for the wolves. There may be some truth to that. Perhaps I was careless. But we shouldn't have to worry about things like that. Shouldn't have to scramble inside as soon as it gets dark. Those animals are getting bolder, and they aren't afraid of us anymore."

"They tricked Kandi. Killed her in broad daylight," Lotta says, looking at Jari for the first time that evening. "They tempted her into the forest, away from me, and then they killed her. When I went after her, they chased me too. Hunted me. In sight of my own home!"

Her words lapse into stifled sobs and are greeted by murmurs from the others in the room. Jari watches the other villagers talk. They're animated, straddling the line between rage and fear. A line he knows well.

Without a word, Steffen steps forward and gently takes the bag from Lotta's hands. She stares at him but says nothing as he zips it up, opens the front door and places it on the porch. The icy blast of outside cuts through the reek of the corpse and Jari breathes easier before he speaks.

"Look at the other things that have happened. Sammi's death. Brought on by the wolves. They stripped his farm to the bone. Killed his herd one by one until he couldn't survive any longer."

"Hold on," Asko says over the din. "You can't pin a suicide on the wolves."

"Tell me they didn't contribute."

"I doubt a coroner would implicate them. Put it that way. How could they? Sammi's farm was in trouble because of Sammi's behaviour. I don't mean to speak ill of the dead, but we all know it. He's been on the brink for years. He couldn't manage his money, and the whole place is falling apart. With or without the wolves taking his herd, Sammi was up the wall financially. And let's not ignore the biggest contributor here: he was probably too drunk half the time to remember to shut in his stock properly. It's not like wolves can open the gates, is it?"

Another mutter from those seated nearest. Asko is the tallest man in the room, and as Jari watches him stand front and centre, he's never felt more intimidated by his friend. Eyes find their way to Jari in this growing game of verbal tennis.

"Those wolves ate Sammi's business alive. Literally. You say it's his own fault. I assume you think Lori being killed and what they did to Kandi was down to people as well. Human error? When in fact, these beasts are bold, and they are cunning. When Lori died, *you* stopped me from going into the forest and killing as many as I could, Asko. You stopped that. Now we're in a position where nobody wants to go out after dark. We're living in fear in our own village. It's time that ended."

"Wolves have always been here. They've had this land longer than us. If anything, we have taken over their territory."

"Bullshit. Yes, they've always been here, but until about a year ago, how many people had actually seen one? Only the hunters. Only those who needed to go into the forest. Now they're bold. Until they're taught to fear us again, they will carry on doing what they want. I saw two in my front yard only a week ago."

"Acting on instinct, no doubt. Acting from the memory of Lori being left out. Looking for easy food. Scavenging. Picking on the weak. That's their nature."

"They're hunting on our lands. Coming for our livestock and our hunting dogs. Where does it end, Asko? With them hunting people's kids?"

"No. We've taken precautions against that."

"Not enough." A voice from the back of the room. Both Jari and Asko look over. Every head in the room turns towards the speaker.

Helenka shuffles into the centre of the room, one hand on the small of her sons' backs, pushing them with her. They drag their feet, teenage boys, all limbs and sulking lips. Their shoulders bunch up around their ears as the men in the room scan them for weakness.

Jari frowns as Helenka takes her place in the middle of the room. He'd always considered Helenka's husband to be a lucky man before he upped and left for Tampere. There had been times at Sammi's barbecues he'd been a few beers deep and thought about making a move on Helenka. Sobering up always brought the shame of realising she was out of his league and the shame of what Magda might've thought about his drunken pass. His lack of respect for Helenka and himself.

But now, in the dim light of his home, he can't believe his eyes. Helenka's face is gaunt. The skin is loose around the eyes and mouth, paler than he remembers. Her hair isn't washed. Instead, it hangs limp, lifeless around her face. The two boys, usually cheeky and full of teenage vitriol, stand silent as if put on pause. Heads bent. He remembers these two asking him for beer at a summer barbecue and slipping them a can apiece. Now, shadows bunch beneath their eyes. All the spirit gone from their faces.

Helenka goes to speak. Her jaw trembles, her mouth a small, dark slash in the white of her face. She shakes her head. One hand goes over her eyes.

"Helenka." Steffen's voice. She looks over at him. "Hels, you can do this."

Hels? Jari thinks.

She breathes deeply, holds it. Bunches her hands into fists by her side. Neither of the boys look at her. "This has to stop," she says, more to the floor than to anyone. "We have to do something about this before someone dies. Before a child dies."

"There's no evidence for that," Asko says, his arm draped over Pia's shoulder.

"There's plenty." She wipes at her cheeks with the back of one hand, head still bent to the floor. "Yesterday morning, a whole pack of them tried to kill my boys."

A wave of whispering and chatter spreads through the room. Everyone speaks at once. It grows into a crescendo and mutes what Helenka says next.

Jari smashes his empty can onto the mantlepiece over and over. "Shut up! All of you. Let her talk."

Eyes still on the floor, Helenka continues.

"I dropped the boys off for the bus. About a hundred yards short of the bus stop. I was running late. There wasn't a chaperone there. It wasn't my day to wait, and I needed to get going." She looks at everyone in the room, her eyes pleading for forgiveness. "I thought they'd be safe in the shelter. The bus wasn't far away. It was only a couple of minutes."

Her voice quavers, and Steffen takes a step towards her but stops. Instead, he makes a show of adjusting his boot and then picks up his beer again. For the first time, Jari notices Maria, Steffen's wife, isn't here.

"They didn't even make it to the bus stop before the first one appeared. In the road behind them. If only I'd seen it in my mirrors. I just didn't … I was too rushed …" She snorts. "Then the others came. Circling. Closing in on the boys. They had no weapons and no help. They decided to run for Steffen's place, the closest house." She wipes her nose on the back of her hand. "They only survived because the bus came a few minutes early. If that driver hadn't made good time, they'd have been …" She trails off into sobs, and her body judders as she tries to hold them in, tries to hold it together in this room full of staring, judging men.

Lotta gets up from her chair and puts an arm around Helenka. She pulls the smaller woman close, and everyone else in the room chooses something else to look at. They fall into silence, eyes on Helenka as she shakes herself free of Lotta's grasp. She looks up, meeting the eyes of those around her, staring first at Steffen and then moving on.

"I'm not a bad mother, if that's what you're thinking. I was in a rush. I was late for work, that's all. I used to live in a nice, safe village where everyone looked out for each other. Now, we barely dare go out after dark without a rifle or a shotgun. These wolves tried to kill my boys. We need to make sure that doesn't happen again."

"I want to hear from the boys," Asko says. "All we've got is hearsay until we hear it from them directly."

"Hearsay? Are you joking, Asko?" Helenka is a coiled spring, bent towards Asko as though ready to pounce. "I told you what happened."

"I'd just like to hear a first-hand account before we do anything rash. I'm being thorough, not judgemental." Pia's grip on Asko's arm tightens. A grimace crosses her pale features as her husband takes on the argument.

"Could've fooled me," Steffen says.

"Boys, are you up to it?" Jari asks.

They look at their mother and then back at Jari. Both nod simultaneously. Mimicking their mother's body language, they stare at the floor. Aware of everyone watching them.

Olaf starts.

"Mum dropped us off and had to go. We made it to the shelter, but I'd seen the one on the road behind us. It wasn't chasing us, but it was sniffing the floor. Smelling us. When I saw it, it just looked at me. Very brave. It wasn't scared. Didn't flinch."

"Then we saw the others," Mikael says. "When we got to the shelter, we saw them in the trees on the banks above the road. They were all barking to each other. We didn't have a choice. We had to run. We had no weapons."

"We ran down the road. They all chased us. We were sliding everywhere on the ice, trying to get to Steffen's house."

"We didn't think we'd make it, but then the bus came, and we got on. If it wasn't for the bus, then they would've got us. No doubt."

There's a silence after they finish speaking. Asko steps forward, blocking Pia from view as he moves closer to the boys. Jari watches him, aware that his friend is a good foot taller than the boys. He knows the feeling.

"What did the bus driver say when you got on?"

"Nothing," Olaf says, looking up at Asko. "We were too out of breath. Too shaken up."

"Did he not see the wolf on the road?"

"No."

"That's a bit strange, isn't it?"

"We were too scared to notice."

"And did you see the wolves from the bus? As you drove away?"

"Not that I remember, but—"

"Not that you remember?"

"It all happened really fast. We were frightened."

Asko makes a show of shrugging to those nearest to him.

"What's that supposed to mean?" Helenka snaps.

"I don't know what you're talking about, *Hels.* I just think it's odd that the only adult on the scene didn't see anything. I called the bus company. Spoke to the driver. He said all he saw was two silly boys running in the middle of the road. Two boys who were incredibly lucky not to be knocked down." He stares down at the boys in front of him, and they shrink under his gaze, folding in on themselves.

"We aren't making it up," Mikael says.

"We aren't," Olaf says. His voice is harder than the last time he spoke.

"Did the wolves approach you before you started running?"

"No. We saw them, and we had to make a break for it." Olaf's face is raised towards Asko's now. Jaw set.

"And how close did they get to you?"

"I didn't see. We were too busy running for our lives to look back."

"So what you're saying is that you can't say for sure."

"I guess so, but we could hear them."

"Hear them. That's all." Asko throws his arms wide as he turns away from the boys and faces the other villagers. Grandstanding like a lawyer in a courtroom drama. "What I'm saying is, there's a big difference between *seeing* a wolf for the first time and being *chased* by a wolf. I think there's a chance that these boys saw a wolf, maybe just one. That they panicked and nearly ended up in a serious accident as a result."

"And I think you're full of shit, Asko." All eyes fall to Helenka. "I think you don't have any kids, so you don't understand what it's like to be so terrified. You don't know what it's like to have to fight to protect your own like this. My boys could've *died.* That's on these wolves. No-one else."

A murmur of approval from the villagers. Jari bends down, fiddles with the cuff of his trousers to hide the smirk on his face at the rollicking Helenka continues to dish out to his friend.

"You've been away for a few years, Asko. Maybe you've gone soft in that time, but you need to look at these people gathered here and remember whose side you're on. It's not us and them; it's us *against* them."

More muttering. Tommi claps from his place wedged into Jari's armchair. An empty can rolls off him and onto the floor. It isn't as though Jari lives like a king, but this is still his home. He bunches his fists as Tommi makes no attempt to pick up the can but doesn't say anything. Tommi barely knows what day it is. There's no point picking a fight with someone like that.

"The thing is," Tommi says, drink blending his words together, "we should be safe to send our children to school without worrying like this."

"Tommi, you don't have any kids," Asko says.

"Thank God," a voice pipes up from the back of the room. Everyone but Tommi sniggers. Some don't pretend to hide it.

"It doesn't matter if they're my kids. They're the village's children. The future of this whole place. We've seen families leave because of money and because they're scared. That never used to happen. At all. Those families have been here for generations. We have to protect our village."

The murmur of approval grows, swelled by Tommi's mutterings. Glasses are clinked together. Cans crushed.

"We've got adequate measures to protect the children. We've got the new buses. We don't let them play out after dark. Who wants to anyway?" Asko says. Beneath his beard, his white teeth are visible as he tries to smile. Aiming for levity. "I think this is an overreaction."

"That bus costs me nearly a hundred euros a month that I can't afford." Helenka snaps. "A while back I used to be able to drop them off nearby on the way to work and know they would walk the rest of the way to school safely. Now, I have to drive out of my way to the bus stop to drop them off. Some days, I have to take my turn and wait with them. My boss gets it, but he's not happy. This is affecting our lives, Asko. You don't understand. At all."

Some of the villagers clap at her words. Tommi mashes his hands together, squinting in concentration as he does. Pia leans towards Asko, whispers in his ear. Asko nods. Tries to smile at her but fails.

"I think the real problem here is that people aren't always acting out of community spirit. I think the issue is that this village wants revenge."

There's a ripple of laughter at Asko's words, but he shrugs, carries on.

"There are people here who have lost dogs to the wolves. There's your motive. The wolves have taken people's livestock. There's your motive. People have to drive out of their way to drop their kids off. You might not like it, but that's your motive. What you're all saying is that, rather than confront what the real problems are here, you'd rather go out and hunt animals with no licence, no plan and no thought of the consequences."

"Nobody's saying that, Asko," Jari says. "But people are scared. Have you been into the forest after dark? It's not a friendly place. Not that it ever was. But it's theirs now.

You can feel it the moment you step outside the door. That's not a good thing."

"I think we're overreacting a bit here. This isn't some fairy tale. We aren't superstitious anymore, are we? Are we afraid of the dark, huddling around our fires and drawing pictures on the walls of our caves?" He laughs, but he's on his own. Even Pia doesn't respond to his attempt at a joke.

"People are losing their livelihoods. It's not just those with herds either. They've been hit the hardest, but hunting is suffering too. The wolves are taking our animals, our dogs. They're limiting our time in the forest."

"It's even scary going fishing," Tommi shouts.

"I don't see the argument about the herds. You own animals and breed them for meat or fur. You're bound to expect some wastage," Asko says.

"Wastage?" Steffen steps forward. "Fucking wastage? Wastage is an animal getting a disease and dying. Not being chased down and ripped to pieces by a pack of wolves. Or have you forgotten what happened to Sammi's elk? The one that tipped him over the edge?"

"It didn't tip him over the edge. It just—"

"Just what? You've got nothing, Asko. What you're suggesting doesn't even make sense. Show them the photos you took."

"I forgot them." Asko bows his head.

"Forgot them? Perfect. You talk of agendas – well what about yours?"

"My agenda is decency and preservation, Steffen. That's what I care about. Everything has its place around here. Even the wolves."

"Fuck off!" Tommi shouts from his chair.

"It's true. Wolves have their place in our ecosystem. They're endangered for a reason. We can't just charge in and start mowing them down. It's a criminal offence. We could go to prison for it."

"No, you wouldn't." At the back of the room, Heiko leans on the frame to the front door. Jari can't remember the last time he saw Heiko without his uniform. His jeans and plaid shirt look alien, as though he's borrowed them from someone else. "I won't let them prosecute you if you cull the wolves. Hell, I'll guarantee it. I'll come too. The police won't be interested."

Asko sighs and rubs at his face with one hand. "This is wrong. If we want to put a stop to the wolf *problem*, then we need to act as a community and act lawfully. I've never said that we shouldn't do something, but what we do has to be right. Right for us and right for the wolves."

"Do the wolves get a fucking vote now? Shall we invite them in, give them a beer and ask their opinion?" Jari asks. The room falls silent.

"No, Jari. They don't get a vote. But you're the best hunter in this village. You know that the whole system round here is finely balanced. If we cull the wolves completely, we'll only create another problem."

"Way I see it, I'd rather have too many elk than too many wolves."

"Hell yeah!" Tommi shouts. Others too shout along. Lotta and Helenka lend their voices to the growing din.

"I'll report this to the government then," Asko says. "Apply for a licence, make them aware of the plans to illegally cull the wolves."

Lotta steps forward, her face twisting as she gets up close to Asko. Her finger jabs into his chest. "Your problem is, Asko, you think you're better than us. With your time in Helsinki and your new wife. You've forgotten what it's like to be down in it with the rest of us. Struggling to make ends meet. You probably describe this place as your holiday cottage to your colleagues. While you're swanning around selling whatever it is and off abroad for holidays. We don't all run a business through a mobile phone. We're suffering. All of us. We don't need you looking down your nose as we try to make things work around here."

"Nobody is looking down their noses," Pia spits. She gets up from her perch on the arm of the sofa and puts herself between Lotta and Asko. Her eyes widen, mouth twisted into a sneer of perfect, white teeth. Asko puts a hand between the two women, steps into the gap, and calms Pia down. Lotta laughs as the married couple mutter between themselves.

Asko turns to Lotta as Pia takes her seat again.

"I was born in this village. Same as the rest of you. I was raised here. A few years in Helsinki don't change that. They don't make me soft. I don't hunt or farm for a living, but that doesn't mean I want to see those ways of life damaged. Me and Pia came here to start our lives over. We want to have children and bring them up here. But we don't want to bring our children up in a community where mob rule takes over. We want this place to be safe and decent, like it was when I grew up here. We don't want our neighbours to have blood on their hands."

"That's bullshit, Asko," Lotta says. "You didn't come back because of that. You came back because your dad died, and you inherited his land. It came free and easy. Just like everything you've got now."

"Nothing comes free and easy, Lotta. You've got no idea what I've been through. You can't even imagine the pressures on me and Pia. Don't put your nose where it doesn't belong, and don't make accusations you can't back up."

Jari swallows as he watches Asko stretch up to his full height. This is the maddest he's seen his friend in at least a decade. A timely reminder that Asko is a man mountain, capable of looking after himself.

"I am of this village. Maybe I make my money elsewhere, but this is still my home, and it always will be. Don't condescend to me because you've never left. Whether it was my father's land or not, me and Pia own property here. We will bring our children up here. We have as much say as anyone. Anyone disagrees with that, they can come and see me outside after this meeting."

Pia steps forward and puts a hand on his arm. He flinches at the touch initially, then puts his arm around her, pulling her close.

"There'll be no need for violence, Asko," Jari says. "We need to put this to the vote. We need to decide on the best way forward for the village."

"All those in favour of applying for a permit to cull a number of wolves in this area, please raise your hands. I'll do all the paperwork and take the application to Helsinki myself if need be. But once they approve it, we will have the full support of the law and the government behind us to look after this community appropriately. Who's with me?" Asko looks round the room, from man to man, woman to woman. A sea of impassive faces.

One hand raises. Pia's.

Jari steps forward, cutting in front of his old friend and his embarrassment. "I propose that Helsinki don't know or care about what goes on out here. They've never cared before, so why should they now?"

Villagers applaud his words.

"The EU need to give us a permit to hunt on our own lands? Not if I have my way."

Tommi puts his fingers in his mouth and whistles.

"The police won't take this any further. We don't have any risks here."

More applause.

"I propose that we get together, all of us—" Jari meets Asko's eye, "—and kill every single wolf we can get our hands on. Cull the whole pack, right down to the juveniles. Get rid of every single one and start over. Take back our lands and our ability to earn a crust. Take back our way of life."

The applause reaches its height, and Jari waves an arm, commanding silence. It falls instantaneously. "Who wants to arrange to cull the wolves? On our terms? Our way?"

Every hand in the room goes up, bar Asko's and Pia's. Even Heiko, over by the door, raises his can towards the ceiling. Tommi cheers and cackles in the armchair. Both Olaf and Mikael look sheepishly at their mother before raising their hands too. Lotta and Helenka add their hands to the group. A clean sweep of votes from the floor. Jari smiles.

"I thought so. I knew it. This place. This village. It's special. We will do something together to keep it that way. To keep this community together."

"Get the beers in," shouts Tommi.

Jari rolls his eyes. "OK, OK. I have some extras in my stores. Let me get them."

As he goes to leave, Pia pushes through the bunched-up villagers. She shoulders into a couple of them, but they're too merry, too giddy at the thought of the cull and free beer to notice. At the door, she stops in front of Jari as he pulls on his boots.

"I hope you're happy. You're ruining this place." Tears make her eyes shimmer, reflecting the light of the room, somehow draining her face of colour. She pushes her dark hair back out of her face. Sets her jaw and looks him in the eye. He's taken aback by the ferocity of her stare.

"We're trying to make the village better and safer for everyone. People's jobs are on the line here. People's lives."

"I grew up in a small village like this. I loved it for so many years. But that community fell apart too. So many big men with their big opinions. They brought that village to its knees. Asko and I love living here. We don't want it ruined."

"We will make it safe. We will make it better. I promise you, Pia."

"This is butchery and nothing more, Jari. Tell my husband to come outside. I'll be waiting in the truck."

She wrenches open the door and marches down the porch steps into the snow. The cold, greedy to suck the warmth from his house, steals in behind her, bringing a handful of snow. He watches her go, waits until she's in the bright red truck, and then heads out to his storage unit at the side of the house.

He roots inside the insulated shed and finds a couple of boxes of bottled beer. He stacks them, feeling the reassuring slosh of liquid inside. Partially frozen beer is a big improvement on totally frozen beer. He locks his shed and turns back to the front of the house. He's aware in that moment that he's alone outside after dark for the first time in months, if not longer. He looks up at the sky, the burning constellations overhead. He struggles to recall the last time he took the time to stare up above. The last time his fear let him out of his own home after dark.

Snow crunches as he makes his way round to the front of the house. The night is still but not silent. Asko leans on the driver's side of the truck, elbows on the sill, his bulk filling the open window. Pia's behind the wheel. Jari stops, not wanting to interrupt. Not wanting to be seen.

"You need to do something, Asko. How can we carry on living here after this? It's a disgrace."

"Calm down. Please." Asko puts a gloved hand on Pia's cheek. "We've got this. We can make it work. This isn't a reason to leave, trust me."

"Feels like a big deal to me. You said you could change Jari's mind."

"And maybe I can. Just give me a chance."

"It's too late now. They've voted. There's no going back. This is your fault. You should've done more."

"I did everything I could." Asko backs away from the truck. "There are too many in there with small minds."

"This is your fault."

"Pia, don't."

Pia slams the truck into gear and wheelspins away, spraying snow behind the clattering tyres. The red lights of the truck disappear into the darkness. Asko stands alone watching them go. Jari keeps his eyes on his friend, his face numbing in the cold, his bare hands cramping beneath the crates of beer.

Asko sighs, his breath escaping in a frozen cloud up into the darkness. He looks round, back at the house. Noise and light spill out of the front door that Jari's left ajar. Another sigh from Asko, and then he climbs the stairs, disappears from view. Jari waits a moment and then follows him in. Warmth spreads across his face and through his fingers as he crosses the threshold.

"About bloody time!" shouts Tommi. "We thought you'd frozen to death."

"Or been eaten by wolves," Heiko adds. Those crowded round Jari laugh and reach in to open the top crate before he's even put them on the table.

Asko stands alone by the fireplace, hands on hips, staring into the burner. Its orange glow flickers, playing shadows across his bearded face. Carving lines that Jari has never noticed before. Aging his friend before his eyes.

Jari cracks a beer and joins in the fun.

***

By the time Jari extricates himself from the conversation, he's tagged another four beers onto his tally for the night. The fire in the burner's been raging the whole time, topped up by people with no care for his woodpile or stores. Sweat hangs from the hairs under his arms, and bunching at the nape of his neck. There are too many people in here still, even though a few have made their excuses. Tommi scolds everyone who leaves from Jari's armchair; he's not moved all night.

Still, Asko sits alone by the fire. The beer he's nursed for the last hour is warm in his hand.

Jari approaches his friend, puts a hand on the big man's shoulder. "I'm sorry this didn't go the way you wanted."

"Are you?" Asko says, eyes still on the fire.

"Of course. I wouldn't change the result, but I know you and Pia are disappointed. It can't be easy for her, being new to our ways and not coming from hunting stock. Can't be easy for you, coming back here and integrating back into the community. I know you've been back a while, but these things take time. We have our own ways here. You know them. You can't change most of these people."

"Most of them? What about you?"

"The difference between me and you is that I like the easy life. You were never going to win that argument, so why try? You can't talk to these people when their dogs and herds are being torn apart. You can't tell people what to think when it comes to the safety of their children."

"You lost Lori. Do you think the cull is wrong?"

"I didn't get my chance at revenge then. I'm more than happy to do it now. You talk about raising kids here. Do you honestly want them to be afraid of the dark? Like some fucking fairy tale? Come on, man. I know you're trying to do a good thing, but you need to see the wider picture."

Asko rubs at his face, thick fingers scratching at his beard.

"We need you, Asko. You're one of the best shots here." Jari lowers his voice. "Look at the rest of them. Tommi can barely move. Heiko works shifts, he's half dead most of the time. We've got a few young lads, Mikka and the like. Steffen's good and Lotta too. But we *need* you to help here." He puts his hand on Asko's arm. "Asko, I need you."

"Pia will never forgive me."

"She will. When she sees the change it will bring to this village. When she sees people happy again. Able to earn money and step outside after dark without worrying. She'll know that we did the right thing. That we did it for everyone. Not just revenge."

"But partly because of revenge."

Jari smiles. Swigs his beer. "It's been a long time coming."

Asko rubs the bridge of his nose. He looks down at Jari. "What's your plan then? Why do you need me?"

"I'm thinking that we lure the beasts out into the forest. Find a clearing. Get a few elk and tie them up."

"A sacrifice?"

"A lure. Some of the farmers have already agreed. One each. We probably need about five in total. A small price to pay in the long term. We'll have shooters in the trees, sniping the beasts as they feed on the elk. Then we have a second on the ground, cleaning up any that escape."

"It's that simple?"

"Of course. It's just an ambush and a clean-up. We've got our people up high, so they're safe when the pack comes, then the people on the ground should only have to take on one or two. Those are safe numbers."

"Safe? Have you ever been face to face with one of these things?"

"Asko, if you're worried, you can be in the first wave. Up high, snipe from a safe distance. I'll be on the ground. Lead by example, eh? Don't worry. We won't be within a hundred yards of one of the things."

"Hmm. That isn't the worst plan. If we're going to do this, it needs to be quick and clean."

"Of course."

"I'll scope the clearing with you."

"If that's what you want."

"And I'll position everyone in the clearing. I'll make sure everyone is safe. Me included."

"That's fine."

"And if Tommi's involved, he's with you."

They both turn and look at Tommi, slumped in the armchair. A wet patch of beer stains his jeans.

"No fucking chance," Jari says.

Asko laughs.

"We need you, Asko. I mean that. Don't let us down."

"I won't. I'm with you, Jari. Not through choice but through necessity. But now you need to promise me something."

"What?"

"When the time comes, none of those animals will suffer. I don't care what you think they've done or what you think they owe you. Clean kills. No pain."

"I'm not a monster, Asko. I just want them gone."

Jari reaches his hand out to shake his friend's. Asko takes it, his grip tight around Jari's hand. Asko smiles with genuine warmth, and Jari feels his shoulders unknot. He tightens his own grip. Nodding his head like he's heard a familiar piece of music.

"What are you going to tell Pia?"

"She'll understand in time. Like you said, she's not from round here. She isn't from hunting stock. We both care deeply about this place, but she's not experienced in this way of life. She'll come around."

"I hope so. She seems good for you."

"She has her moments." Asko smiles. "That's the thing about her: she's fiery. Keeps me on my toes."

"I remember that feeling. I, erm, well … doesn't matter."

"What?"

Jari lowers his voice. "I caught sight of the photo of Magda earlier. Got me thinking about what she'd think of the cull. Whether she'd support me or you."

"She always had a soft spot for me, Magda. She was too kind, too generous."

"That's what I always told her. Told her you were our friend, not our son."

"She'd have been a wonderful mother."

Jari doesn't say anything at first. Just stares into the flames, can in hand.

"I just hope she'd understand what I'm trying to do," he says eventually. "Why this place is so important."

"She would, Jari. Absolutely she would."

Feeling the presence of everyone still here in his home, drinking their way through his supplies – thinking how he'd trade all of them, even Asko, for one more day with Magda – he finishes the last of his lager. It leaves a tinny, metallic taste on his tongue. He crushes the can and sets it on the mantelpiece, aware of Asko watching him. He turns to his friend and jerks his thumb towards the other men in the room.

"Come on. Let's get involved."

He turns to the men, clears his throat until they stop chattering and turn to look at him. "You're never going to believe it, but guess who's come round?"

"No way," Steffen cackles.

"What about that wife of yours?" Heiko asks.

"She's learned to live with me missing the toilet bowl when I piss. She'll learn to live with this. Don't you worry," Asko replies.

Jari catches Asko's eye as the others collapse into laughter. There's no humour to his friend's face despite his words. Jari slaps him on the shoulder.

"Come on, big man, let's get a few more in."

***

Asko is the last to leave. Heiko had herded the others out and into his truck a few minutes before. The police officer drank at least as much as the others. Nobody raised an objection when he snatched up his keys and announced he was leaving.

They didn't offer Asko a ride home. Instead, they piled into the truck and headed off home in the opposite direction to where Asko lives.

Jari sits alone with the big man now, both on the sofa. More than a few beers into the session and in danger of running dry again.

Hassa snores on the carpet under the coffee table. Empty cans litter every surface of the house. The kitchen is peppered with empty glasses and cups and plates. Jari wrinkles his face at the sight of the cleaning to be done. All of it could wait. His head's already starting to thud with a premature hangover. It's as though his eyes are no longer connected, able to move independently of each other. His vision swims and then settles.

Next to him, Asko rests his head on one hand, as though propping it up. "I can't remember the last time we drank this much together," Asko says.

"I can," Jari's words run together. "It was the wake. Magda's wake."

"I'm sorry, Jari."

"S'OK." Jari waves a hand as though wiping away the grief in front of his face. "Not your fault."

"I need to go. Can I ask you something first?"

"What?"

"Will you change your mind about the cull?"

Jari laughs and slops beer across the sofa from his can. "Good one, Asko." But when he turns to his friend, he sees there's no trace of a smile on Asko's face. The solemnity of his friend's face sobers him a touch. "You're serious? You've just spent the evening telling everyone you'll help. What the fuck are you doing?"

"I will help, assuming I can't change your mind now."

"You can't."

"We don't have to do this, Jari. You're the best hunter we have, people know that. They'll listen to you."

"But this needs to be done, Asko. It must happen. You heard what happened to those boys. Next thing you know, it'll be a person we find torn to pieces. It could be anyone."

"You could change your mind. You'd lose face at first, Steffen would hit the roof, but they'd come round. A lot of what happened tonight was just posturing."

"You've waited until I've had however many beers, and now you're trying this? Do you think you can trick me? Change my mind while I'm drunk?"

"I've waited until we're alone. It's not my fault you've had so much to drink."

"And now we're pointing fingers?"

"No. I've matched you, beer for beer. There's just a lot more of me. That's all. Look, Jari. You should think on this, sleep on it, whatever. It's all well and good being the leader when everyone's had a few drinks and their bloodlust is up. But tomorrow, you're going to wake up in the cold with a splitting headache. Everything will be clear then. The detail. The planning. The risk. You need to look at it all and decide if this is still what you want."

"Don't talk down to me, Asko. We're all grown men. We've made our decisions. You lost out. You need to accept it. How would you feel if you won out and then someone died?"

"That won't happen."

"You can't say that. Someone has already nearly died, those two boys!"

"Those two boys saw a wolf and panicked. It's not the same thing."

"I don't want to hear this again, Asko. You were in favour of a government-sanctioned cull. Now you're talking like you don't want a one of them to die. You can't have either of those options. You have to accept what's happened."

"I do. I just don't want to give up on the people in this village until I have to."

"What's that supposed to mean?"

"It'll be hard for us to live here. Hard for us to look our neighbours in the face knowing that they don't agree with our views. It'll be hard for Pia to look at me, knowing what I've done. What I've been involved with."

"You're in this now, Asko. You'll be hounded out of here if you drop out, and you know it."

Asko nods and Jari cuts across him.

"Pia will be angry short term, but she'll come round once she sees the benefit to the village. People have short memories. In a few years, none of this will matter."

"And if Magda had been against this cull?"

"She would've kept quiet and let me get on with what's best for everyone."

Asko sighs. "I'd better go. I've tried everything I can to get out of this. Now I'll have to try everything I can to keep Pia calm and see what happens."

"She'll come round."

Asko gets up and begins the process of getting ready to leave. He pulls on his two coats, gloves, hat and finally, his boots. He walks across the room, slaps Jari on the back and pulls him from his vigil watching Hassa sleep.

Jari jerks and gets to his feet. "You need a ride home?"

"You're joking! How many beers have you had?"

"Getting in the truck with me is safer than walking home in the dark."

"Now I know you've had too many. I'll walk."

"Asko, you can't. It's pitch black."

Asko pulls out a torch from his coat pocket, shines the light in Jari's face and laughs as he recoils from the beam.

"I don't mean you're scared of the dark," Jari says, rubbing the bridge of his nose. "What about the wolves?"

"I'll be fine."

"It's a half-hour walk back to yours. It's too risky."

"I'm not afraid, Jari. I don't live in fear like you. The walk will sober me up."

"Well, if you won't accept a ride, then at least borrow a rifle."

"Seriously, Jari. Calm down. I'll be fine. I'm not afraid of them."

"Famous last words. I'll be reminding you of that when they're stitching your arms back on in the hospital."

"Goodnight, Jari."

Asko has a hand on the door by the time Jari is off the sofa and close enough to stop him.

"I know what you're risking for this cull, Asko. You're a good man."

Asko looks down at Jari, then pulls the smaller man into a brisk hug. Jari slaps Asko on the back again. From under the coffee table, Hassa wakes and begins to yap.

"Come on then, you dozy thing." Asko slaps his thighs, and Hassa scuttles over, jumping up as Asko pets her.

Jari scoops Hassa up as Asko opens the door. Cold air floods Jari's lungs. Winter burns into his chest. Hassa struggles in his arms, desperate to get free.

"Goodnight, Asko. Be safe."

On the steps, Asko turns and salutes his friend, his coat bright yellow in the light from the porch. Jari looks past his friend, frowning into the shadows and blackness beyond the porch's meagre lighting. He watches Asko trudge through the powder, grateful on his friend's behalf that there's no snow falling. Asko disappears into the dark, and hairs rise on Jari's arms. He grips Hassa tighter and shuts the door, puts the dog down, and fastens the three bolts.

Once alone and secure, he ignores the mess and slumps back onto the sofa. The last beer in the crate whispers to him, and he cracks the can open, unperturbed by the can being warm to the touch. He clicks on the TV and starts the sitcom DVD, letting the familiarity of the theme tune and the warmth of his dog calm his thundering heart.

Chapter Eight

Early morning, too early. They congregate at Jari's house again. They swagger in as one, exchanging handshakes and slapping each other's backs. They crowd into Jari's small kitchen, all bluster and bullshit. Lotta arrives alone. She puts her rifle down by the door and takes a seat in silence, shoulders slumped.

Asko arrives last, on foot despite the early start and cloak of darkness that still drapes itself over the forest. Jari takes this to mean that Pia still hasn't forgiven him for what he's about to do. Yet Asko is himself from the moment he opens the door, teasing the others and joining in.

Playing host again, Jari cooks for them. The kitchen quickly fills with the sizzle of the frying pan. They cram around his pitiful kitchen table, some sitting, some standing. All of them stuff themselves with plates of blood sausage, bacon and scrambled eggs. Locusts devouring his stores for the second time in a week.

Jari watches as they gorge, scrapping over the last pieces of his offering while he picks at his own breakfast. His stomach churns. His senses are dulled and distant from lack of sleep. Tommi chats incessantly, his mouth full. The others joke and jostle as though they're about to head out on an all-day drinking session. He catches Lotta's eye over her full plate. She's shrunk since Kandi's death. Shrivelled. He knows how she feels. He's been there. She looks back down at her food, pushes it away. The others dive into the scraps.

When they've eaten, Asko gathers the dishes and places them in the sink, soaking them in hot water. Jari is grateful to his friend. Already this day is stretching out before him. Tommi mutters something about Asko being under Pia's thumb but doesn't repeat it when Asko looks at him.

"Jari," Asko says, taking his seat and deliberately leaning a shoulder into Tommi, "you came up with this plan. You pick the teams."

"We're not playing tug of war here," Lotta says. "It's time that you got your heads in the game. This is serious."

Even Tommi falls silent. Jari hides his smirk behind his coffee mug. Lotta's words crystalise the air. The gravity of the situation.

"As I've said, two groups. One to go ahead and snipe from the trees. This group will likely do most, if not all of the killing. The second group will come in on the ground and sweep up any stragglers left alive. Think of it as a clean-up crew.

"Asko will lead the sniping. He's one of the better shots from long range. He knows the forest."

Jari looks around, waiting for one of the others to say something or to make their run at taking Asko's place. Nobody meets his eye.

"Good. I'll lead the clean-up crew. This is the most dangerous place to be. If the first team leave too many wolves, we'll likely be one on one with them. Anyone who can't handle that needs to leave now. You will get your hands dirty today. Mark my words."

Again, he eyes those in the room. Nobody looks at him, but nobody dissents. He takes this as agreement.

"Asko, you take Mikka, Tommi and Heiko. You've already picked the spots. Don't waste any time. Get set up early and be patient. They'll come."

Asko shoots a sideways look of disdain at Tommi but nods at Jari.

"I'll take Steffen, Lotta, Ivan and Mixu. There's more of us because we may need more firepower on the ground."

Rolling up his sleeve, Asko checks his watch. Its digital face flashes into life. He frowns. "We'd better get going."

He gets up. The rest of his team follow. They don their outdoor clothes over the top of their thermals, pulling on coats and gloves, boots and hats. Weapons are snatched up and checked, checked again.

Tommi starts to moan about his fear of heights. Asko tells him to shut up as he strides over to Jari.

"You got this, Asko?"

"You're in safe hands. Just come prepared to put an end to this." Asko leans in towards Jari, a head taller than his friend. Jari feels like a little boy in comparison. Small. Pathetic. "Remember. Keep this humane."

"Of course. We'll see you soon."

They leave without another word. Heiko's truck bursts into life outside and disappears into the gathering dawn. All that's left for Jari's team is to wait. He turns back from the window and looks at them. Good men who he's known for years. Men he can rely on. He classes Lotta in this. She's at least as capable as the others, if not more. Despite the growing awkwardness between them, she's reliable and cautious.

His team sits in silence. The camaraderie and the banter from breakfast has evaporated. The enormity and danger of their task sinks in, settling into their minds. Conversation is culled. Hassa lies on the sofa, eyes closed, leg twitching as she dreams.

Jari lets them sit like this for as long as he can stand it. Then he pulls himself away from the window, starts getting ready, and invites the others to do the same.

***

They drive in silence to the rendezvous spot. Only the rumble and clink of the chained wheels over frozen ground interrupt the silence. Jari can't think of anything to say to break the silence's hold over them, as though he's forgotten every word he's ever known. The rest of them stare out of the window or at their hands. Nobody looks at each other. Each are lost to their own thoughts.

Dawn claims the forest as they park up. Heiko's truck sits next to the cattle trailer they used for transporting the elk. The shaped steel looks out of place in the majesty of nature. Stunted grey light breaks over the trees. Enough light to see, still dark enough for the wolves to remain active. Timed to perfection. Jari watches the sky for a few seconds, thanking Asko for calculating this correctly.

Adrenaline rises through him as they trek to the clearing. Snow mutes their movements, slowing them down into the bargain. They press on through the powder, working harder now, their breath fogging around them. Eagerness and confidence spurs them on. Jari, at the head of the group, feels a growing certainty in the plan.

His plan.

Snow tinted the same grey as the sky stretches out ahead of them. Every shadow is a charcoal sketch, long, dark lines resisting the morning to the last. Jari looks around them constantly, head on a swivel. There is no pack tracking them, no outlier waiting to alert the others. Asko's crew has left little sign of their own journey to the clearing. Even if the wind changes, Jari feels it'll make no difference now. Most of the wolves will be dead.

Once they settle into the rhythm of the hike, they make good progress. Without dogs to wrangle or keep quiet, their progress is straightforward. Jari cocks his head as he hears a sound. Clenches a fist and raises it. Behind him, the others stop dead.

Uninhibited by anything else, the sound blossoms in the stillness of the dawn air. The low bass note of a moose calling out. Pain on its voice. It stops abruptly, leaving one second of silence before a new sound replaces it: the unmistakable howl of a wolf. Sustained and cutting. Despite his adrenaline and his layers, cold tickles Jari's spine.

He waves a hand to his team, and puts his head down, surging forward towards the clearing.

***

As they near the clearing, the wolf's howl circles them in the air – interrupting their thoughts, egging them on. Jari springs through the snow in clumsy strides, carving up the knee-high powder. Breath hangs in front of his face. Lungs burning.

There's an epileptic bleat from one of the sacrificial animals. Frantic and fearful. A low roar and another howl. Then a crash of silence as the howls stop simultaneously. Jari smiles. Asko's team are doing their job.

With a wave, he tells his team to fan out. They keep pace with him, in a line together now, ready to sweep into the clearing. He clutches his weapon in gloved hands. Nothing provides reassurance in the wilderness like a gun. Out here, it is the difference between life and death. Everyone attending today is holding an automatic rifle. They've been told to bring their newest, most powerful weapon. There will be no jamming and no misfires.

They are ready to end this.

As one, the five of them pour into the clearing, all from different angles. Rifles raised. Scopes set. Fingers on triggers, ready to bring death to anything that threatens them.

In the deep, grey light, there is nothing but remains.

Jari hears one of the others gag. It doesn't matter who.

The clearing is a replica of the moose hunt. Exposed bones cracked and bent. Tangled, matted fur. Sodden red snow. Branches and scrub caked in steaming blood and ligaments. Bodies stripped clean of meat.

By his feet, a solitary eye stares up at Jari from a moose's skull, judging him.

Jari looks around the clearing, deserted but for the carnage of hunger. The others stop dead, bodies already slumping as adrenaline ebbs away. Jari doesn't know how, but the wolves are gone. They fell into the trap, the scent of the moose and the elk too much for them to resist. Yet they had still shaken their noose. He scans the detritus, desensitised to the violence after his prior experience. He kicks idly at a thigh bone. It rings hollow.

There are no wolf corpses amongst the remains.

"Where the fuck are they?" Steffen asks, pulling his balaclava away from his face.

"Something must have spooked them," Mixu says. His eyes are on Jari. "We lost composure on the approach. Made too much noise."

"Oh, this is my fault, is it?" Jari turns square to Mixu, smirking behind his balaclava as he realises he's got a couple of inches on the younger man.

"Stop measuring your dicks and get your head in the game." Lotta's voice rings through the clearing, annoyance on every syllable. "Look at the state of this. Look what they've done. This isn't nature. This is evil."

She kneels by one of the skeletons. Its ribs grab up at the grey sky like hollow fingers. Her eyes widen behind her balaclava, pools of white inside the knitted black.

"None of this would've happened if we'd planned this ambush properly." Mixu says. "Now look what's happened. The fucking wolves are gone."

"We did plan it. Me and Asko planned it all out." Jari says. His lips barely move as he speaks. His words are a growl.

"Could've fooled me," Mixu says. "Maybe you're just not as good as everyone makes out."

Jari looks over to where Lotta is crouched, eyes fixed on the bones and sinew in front of her. In his peripheral vision, he sees Mixu follow his line of sight. Without a word, Jari steps towards the younger man and plants an uppercut onto Mixu's chin. Mixu staggers, then slumps sideways into the snow. Jari is on him immediately, rifle discarded, knees on the younger man's chest. One gloved hand on Mixu's throat. The other raised to deliver further justice.

Shouts fill the air. Strong arms grip Jari from behind. Steffen's breath is hot in his ear as curses fill his brain. Crimson covers everything, and he wrestles against Steffen and Ivan. In that moment, there's no thought in his mind other than to kill. The rage against the insult. The humiliation of his plan failing. Right at that second, a bullet in Mixu's face would make it all go away.

Steffen's face fills Jari's field of vision. "Calm the fuck down, Jari."

"This isn't my fault."

"Calm down."

"All right. All right."

Lotta is still making her way through the killing floor, shaking her head as she goes – whether at what she's finding or at his behaviour, it isn't clear. Jari senses that door is forever closed to him now. Her friendship is gone. Mixu is alone. On his feet now but groggy. Jari's rifle lies in the snow between them.

Jari shakes himself loose of Ivan and Steffen, steps forward and snatches up his rifle from the powder. He shakes the snow from it and cocks it. He looks over at Mixu and then turns away.

Steffen slaps him on the shoulder. "Come on. Keep it together. Maybe we can fix this."

"How?"

"Track them."

"No, no. This was set up to be our terrain. Our trap. We can't go following them to fuck knows where. We'll lose our advantage."

Ivan leans in. "Where are the others? Did they even make it?"

From her position in the centre of the massacre, Lotta lets out a low moan. "Oh Jesus. Oh shit. Oh Jesus."

"What is it?" Jari shouts.

"Come here. All of you."

They do as they're told and weave their way through the worst of the mess to where Lotta is stood. Mixu brings up the rear, deliberately hanging back. Lotta rolls up her balaclava, her face a colour beyond white. She doesn't say anything. Instead, she points to the floor. To the nearest pile of bones.

A human arm lies in the snow, stripped of its skin. Muscle and sinew exposed. A shattered digital watch hangs limply from the exposed bone.

"Oh shit. It's Asko's!" Jari hears the tremble to his words but can't stop it.

They all start to talk at once. All shouting. Voices bounce off the trees around them.

"Shut up!" Lotta shouts. Her voice is piercing. They all fall silent. "Look."

Beyond the arm lie the ruins of other bodies. Torn shreds of clothing. Rifles, discarded and useless. Bones exposed in shredded trousers. A boot with an ankle bone protruding. Tommi's corpse lies on its side, back to them. Jari reassumes control of the group, steps forward and rolls him onto his back. Tommi's body is a cavity, void of any organs. His dark eyes stare up at the sky. Lifeless.

Ivan lets out a low moan. "They're all dead. All of them."

"How the fuck did this happen?" Jari's hands are over his face, yet he can't remember moving them.

"They were armed." Lotta says. "This is what the wolves are like. They're cunning. I told you all."

Steffen snatches his rifle from his shoulder. "We've got to do something. Follow them. We can't hang back. Not now they've killed four of our own."

Jari can't think. Can't follow what's being said. His thoughts buzz like a swarm of bees bouncing off the insides of his skull. He takes a breath. Lets the cold flow through him, chilling his thoughts, making them manageable.

"Fuck this. Those vermin have killed our friends. Let's track them down and finish them." He turns to Lotta, still standing furthest into the ruin of humanity. "Are there tracks?"

Lotta turns, scouring the snow for clues. She turns back, pointing to the far side of the clearing.

"Yes, they headed out that—"

A bullet zips through the air. The side of Lotta's head explodes in a burst of red. Her body stays upright for a second before toppling backwards into the blood and snow.

More bullets power through the cold air. Steffen is next. Then Ivan. Then Mixu. All dropped by headshots. None of them able to make a sound before death takes them.

It's Jari's turn. A muffled pop and his left knee is nothing but agony. Blood gushes from the wound, and he gags as he sees a flash of white bone beneath. He collapses into the sodden snow, on his side in the blood of his friends.

Everything is pain.

His gloved hands hold his shattered knee, as though stopping it from coming apart further. Fogged breath clouds his vision as he pants. His pain is physical in the air around him.

Off to the side of the clearing, there's a shuffling sound. A scraping against wood. Then the crunch of footsteps in powder. His rifle lies a few feet away. He reaches an arm out in vain, unwilling to move it too far from his shattered knee. The muzzle watches his efforts, like a blank eye, dispassionate.

The crunching gets nearer. Stops a few feet away. There's the snap of a rifle being cocked. Jari looks up, squinting through the pain.

"I won't bother helping you up. You're likely in too much pain anyway."

"Asko?" Jari grunts. "What the fuck have you done? Those men, Lotta, they're your friends. Our friends. I'm your friend."

Asko watches his friend down the scope of the gun, keeping it raised and trained on Jari's face.

"I know, Jari. And it's you being here that hurts me most. Of all the people who helped us when Pia and I moved back to the village, you were the most kind. It was like I'd never been away."

"Why have you done this? Have you gone insane?"

"We needed this new life so badly, Jari. It's a shame you had to get in the way. We really wanted you to be part of this new society. This new order. I gave you enough chances, Jari. More chances than Pia wanted to give you. All I wanted to hear was that you'd changed your mind."

Jari cries out in pain. "If you're going to kill me, just do it. Please. This is agony."

"I'm not going to do that. If *I* wanted you dead, you'd already be the same as the others."

"Asko, please. Help me."

"It's not for me to help you now. You made your choice. All of you. You chose blood and violence. Well, these things can go both ways. As you're about to find out. Goodbye, Jari."

Asko steps past Jari and reaches into the gore to retrieve his watch. He tilts the cracked screen towards the light and shrugs, drops the battered watch into his pocket. Keeping his rifle trained on Jari, Asko backs away from his friend, step by step. His eyes look somewhere beyond Jari's prone form. Jari tries to turn but can't move without shooting pains in his leg.

"Where are you going?"

Asko doesn't answer. He keeps moving backwards.

The trees around the clearing then come alive with movement. Wolves flow between the gaps in the trees. Moving silently. Stalking. Heads bowed. Senses on high alert. Their eyes gleam in the growing light – some vivid shades of yellow, others a shocking blue. All trained on Jari.

Their languid bodies glide over the snow, unhurried and assured. None of the wolves pay Asko any attention. They weave around him as though he is just another tree in their path. Asko doesn't flinch as they brush by. Their snouts are livid red, dripping wet and sharp.

The wolves step over the bodies of the murdered men and Lotta. More forbidden meat for them to feast on later. Jari looks at the blown-open heads and wonders how Asko could do this to people he'd known for years. How could he sit by and watch others get torn to pieces in his rifle sights and do nothing?

"It's their territory now, Jari," Asko says. "Their village. There's nobody left to defend it. No hunters. No killers. People who can be talked round or brought to heel. They can be disposed of if needs be."

"Don't do this."

"It's the only way."

"Shoot me. Kill me now, Asko. Please."

"I'm sorry. It's not for me to make the kill. You organised this cull, Jari. You brought everyone together. They think you're the alpha in the village. It's them you have to answer to."

"Asko! Asko!"

Asko shakes his head and turns, racing full pelt towards the shadows that still cling between the trees. His grey jacket disappears into the darkness as he runs.

"Fuck you! Fuck you, Asko!"

Jari drags himself towards his rifle. Fingers scrape through the powder. His ruined leg refuses to do anything he asks. Snow touches his exposed bone, and he screams. His face sags into the snow, but he still tries to keep moving.

The wolves are on him before he even gets close to the rifle.

The first wolf looks at him for a second. Unmoving. Its yellow eyes calculating. Then it bites down on his outstretched arm. Its teeth fail to get any purchase through his thermal layers and jacket. It throws its head from side to side, shaking itself loose.

This isn't so bad.

Another wolf pushes through and sinks its teeth into the soft meat of his face and neck. Its teeth rip at the ligaments and veins along his jawline. Jari screams, and his jaw extends further than it should. One side slips free and hangs down. Blood pours down his neck and onto the snow beneath him.

Other wolves dart forward and sink their teeth into his limbs and back. There's nothing but fur and blood in his vision. There's no time to react. No vision of Magda's face before him. No thoughts other than pain.

The largest wolf steps forward. Sleek and steel grey. Its eyes electric blue. Somehow familiar. Jari tries to break free. His fingers brush the strap of his rifle. Every movement makes the wolves' teeth tear his flesh wider, pulling himself apart.

The wolf takes its time and moves behind him, out of his line of sight. He feels its movements as it positions itself to his side. He tries to struggle, but it's pointless. He's outnumbered. Incapacitated. The wolf's breath is hot and fetid on the back of his head. The stench of meat and murder. Its teeth are daggers in his flesh as they enter.

The wolf twists.

Jari hears the bones in his neck crack, and then everything is nothing.

***

The wolves let go of their positions and pour forward, snarling and barking as they fight to tear through his outer clothing and into the sweet flesh below.

The sound of tearing and yelping fills the clearing as the wolves taste the spoils of their victory.

Chapter Nine

Steam engulfs him in the shower, holding him in its warm embrace. He presses his forehead against the tiles, reassured by their solidity as though they are the only thing that can hold him up. The jets of hot water ease the tension and aches in his neck and back. He rolls his shoulders, feeling them come alive.

Taking down a nail brush from the shelving unit, he scrubs at his cuticles until he can't take the pain any longer. It's a pointless act. There was never any blood on his hands.

Not literally.

All physical trace of the day is gone from his skin. As he shuts off the water, he hears Jari's shouts rattle through his thoughts. The chill air of the bathroom jolts the sound from his mind. As he dries himself, he worries the mental stain of the day may take much longer to scrub clean than the physical ones.

***

She's waiting for him in the bedroom. He stumbles through the door. Every muscle aches, reverberates with the deep need to shut down. He wants nothing more than to shut down. To not to have to think. He cracks his neck from side to side, trying to loosen the tension. Trying not to think of the exposed and broken bones lying in the clearing.

She pushes her dark hair from her face. Her skin is pale. Her blues eyes shine even under the bright, electronic lights.

"You were a long time there, my husband."

"I had a lot of dirt to wash away. A lot of things to get straight. I still don't feel clean." He brings his fingers close to his face, inspecting the seams of his knuckles and beneath his fingernails.

"Maybe some of it will never truly wash away, Asko. You may have to live with that. We both will." Their eyes meet. "You impressed me today, just as you always do. You've done everything I could ever ask and more."

"Thank you, my love. Everything I do is for you. I do it all for this family."

"The moment I met you, I saw your inner strength. I knew you would be my man. The man who could help us shape this world into something better than it is."

He walks to the bed, leans over and kisses her. His towel falls loose from his waist, and she smiles.

"You're the most beautiful woman I've ever seen. The second I saw you, I was yours."

"What a world we have created today. A place that is safe for this family of ours." She guides his hands to her belly, over the top of her clothing. "This child has its father's power."

"Hopefully, its mother's beauty."

"This village is safe now. The women and children will fall in line. We have the privacy we need. We can live our way. The old way. The true way."

He kisses her, and she pulls him down on top of her. Her hands caress his body. He tugs at her clothes, and she helps him, undressing quickly. Clothes fall from the bed to the floor. He moves his hands over her body, exploring the sinewy strength of her. Fingers glide over the matting of hair that covers most of her skin. Her eyes open wide at his touch. A shock of blue. Somewhere between the lupine and the human. Hers is that same bestial scent that has always drawn him in. Aroused him deeper than any woman he's ever known. How she straddles the line between wolf and woman, human and beast. She's alluring and repulsive.

His dream and his waking nightmare.

The queen of the world that he has created for her.

He enters her, and she grunts, a low growl in her throat. He moves faster, and her teeth find his shoulder for a taste of his flesh.

She growls louder. More bestial.

Finally, she lets out a groan of pleasure, rising in pitch and urgency.

And from the forest around their small home, the noise is echoed with a chorus of howls.

Acknowledgements

As with every book, there are a number of people to thank for their help and their support.

Firstly, to Kev Harrison and Grant Longstaff. Thanks for reading this novella in its various forms over the years. Without your enthusiasm for the story, it never would've made it this far. It's appreciated more than you know, lads.

Thanks to Paul M. Feeney for reading this story as a 4,000 word short story about five years ago (probably more). Your comments helped me to figure out that this was too much story for such a short word count.

Thanks as ever to those writers who have inspired me and continue to let me cling to them for knowledge and comfort. Thanks to Michael David Wilson and Andrew David Barker. Also thanks to Luke Kondor, Daniel Willcocks, John Crinan and everyone else in the Hawk & Cleaver gang. The podcast chat keeps me going!

A massive thank you to Dave Jeffery for providing such an incredible blurb for this book and also for being one of the most selfless and kind people in the genre. Dave's help with promoting my work and that of others has been invaluable in the year or so since *Dark Missives* launched. It is massively appreciated.

Another huge thank you to Simon Bestwick (Daniel Church) for his generous words on the cover and in

ACKNOWLEDGEMENTS

private. Coming from a writer that I've always admired, those words mean the world to me.

This book wouldn't have happened without the fantastic work of Paul Stephenson at Hollow Stone Press on the cover, the design, and just general publishing knowhow. The man is not only a Photoshop genius but a bloody good human as well. Thanks, sir.

Lastly, the eternal thank you to my girls, Jen and Elsie. I know I'm a grumpy old sod when I'm in the middle of a story and even worse when I'm not, but you both light me up like nothing else. Your love and support make all of this possible. Without you, I'd be nothing. It's all for you both.

About The Author

Dan Howarth is a writer from the North of England.

Dan has also released *Dark Missives* (a collection of short stories) and *Lionhearts,* his upcoming novel from Grey Matter Press.

Dan's short fiction has featured in *Weird Horror Magazine* and on *The Other Stories* podcast numerous times.

Like all Northerners, Dan enjoys rain, pies and drinking blood from the skulls of his enemies.

www.danhowarthwriter.com

Also By Dan Howarth

Dark Missives is the debut collection from author Dan Howarth, bringing together eleven stories that encompass the full range of horror.
Let Dark Missives take you on a tour of the roads less travelled in Northern England to discover what truly lies in the shadows.

Printed in Great Britain
by Amazon